MURDER AUDIT

A CYNTHIA WEBBER NOVEL

MICHELLE CORNISH

For the brave men and women fighting for their land all over the world.

For my readers.

ACKNOWLEDGMENTS

A special thanks to my beta readers: Kay, Kris, Nancy, and Scott. Your feedback was invaluable and made *Murder Audit* better than it was.

Thanks to Dee for your patience and skill, and to my mom, Kay, for having eagle eyes when mine were seeing only what I wanted to see.

To my writing coaches, Alexa Bigwarfe and Kevin T. Johns: Without your advice and inspiration, *Murder Audit* would still be an incomplete draft. Thank you!

1

It was New Year's Eve and Jim Dunn, Controller of Prairie Pipeline Co. (PPC), had no plans. He rubbed his eyes as he glanced up at the clock on the wall of his office. It was almost 7:00 p.m., and while this would be an early night for him, he was ready to call it quits. He had been working late hours preparing for PPC's annual financial statement audit, and he wanted to make sure everything was in order for tomorrow's inventory count. Although he had met with the audit manager, Cynthia Webber, several weeks ago, he felt it was important he was at the office bright and early on inventory day.

He reached into his desk drawer and pulled out a half-full bottle of Crown Royal. He unscrewed the cap and poured a good jigger into his stale, cold coffee. After replacing the bottle in his desk drawer, he swirled his coffee cup and downed the concoction in three big gulps. As he planted his cup back on his desk in its usual spot, he thought he heard voices. Knowing he was alone in the office, he went to the window and noticed some protestors had gathered outside the front entrance. Feeling brave from his last three mugs of "coffee Royal," he opened his window and shouted at the protesters.

"Get outta here you granola loving hippies! You realize this town wouldn't be what it is today without this company. I bet half of you have friends who work for us. Go find something better to do!" As Jim closed the window, he heard something thunk against the building. He looked at the angry mob of about 20 to see they were throwing rocks at his window. He opened the window again, muttering under his breath while rolling his eyes.

"I'm calling the police!"

"Oooh, the police. We're scared now!" one of the protesters sarcastically snapped back. Jim was angry and ready to take matters into his own hands. He was sick and tired of environmental protest groups showing up at the office and disturbing not only the normal course of business but also the time he put in after hours. It was almost as if they were stalking him. He just couldn't understand why they would choose 7:00 p.m. on New Year's Eve as a time to protest. Then he remembered there was a benefit dinner and dance at the University to raise funds to relocate the hundreds of thousands of birds that would be without homes if the new pipeline went in just south of the city.

Jim opened the front door to PPC. Now face to face with the mob, he felt like it had doubled in size in the time it took him to get from his office to the front door. He paused, feeling a little smaller than he had from the safety of his office. He wished he had stopped to call the police like he'd threatened. He started waving his hands around yelling for the crowd to disperse.

"Just go home. We can find another way to resolve this. Your protesting doesn't accomplish anything." Jim panicked as he saw that many of the protestors still had rocks in their hands. He wondered just how angry the mob was and whether they would have the nerve to throw the rocks when face to face with another human. There were empty beer cans littered on the ground, and Jim still had enough sense about him to realize there was no predicting what this mob might do. As he turned to head into the office for cover, he noticed a woman who didn't look like she belonged. He recognized her but couldn't remember from where. She looked beautiful in her fancy red dress.

Jim reached for the keypad to the office door which had locked behind him when he came out to confront the protestors. Whack! He felt a sharp burning pain at his temple as he fell to the snow-covered ground. Jim tried to get up but couldn't. Everything was cold and dark around him. He could hear voices but couldn't tell where they were coming from. They sounded far away.

"Shit, shit, shit! What do we do now?" he heard a woman's voice.

"Just go. Go to your fancy benefit thing. The rest of us will take care of this. Why did you even come here tonight?" a man replied.

"I was trying to be supportive. He's going to be okay, right? I'll call 9-1-1."

"9-1-1? Are you friggin' insane? We'll all get arrested."

"He needs help; there's so much blood."

"You hit him in the head. Head wounds bleed a lot. He'll be fine. We'll clean up this mess then call 9-1-1 on our way out of here. Just go, get out of here!"

"You swear you'll call 9-1-1?"

"Yes! Now go, before your colleagues wonder where you are, or some camera crew shows up and catches you on video." The woman felt something fall from her ear as she turned to leave. She touched her naked ear and looked down at the ground, hoping to find her crystal earring. The ground was bare. She bent down to have a closer look.

"What are you doing? I said get out of here!"

"Alright, alright. I'm sorry I came!" she yelled back. She reached up to the ear where the crystal earring remained, removed it, and tucked it in her purse. When she got back to her car, she glanced back at the mob and saw that many of them were starting to leave.

All Jim wanted to do was go to sleep, but he felt so cold. He could feel his warm blood trickling down his temple and into his ear. He felt his breathing getting shallower, and his heart beat slowing. He feared if he drifted off, he wouldn't wake up. Jim sensed he was being carried. He tried to focus on the sounds around him but couldn't hear anything. Someone had a hold of his arms, and he could feel a tight grip around his ankles.

"Let's put him in there."

"Are you kidding? I don't understand why we didn't just leave him where he was?"

"At least here he'll be under cover. Since we can't get into the office, this is the next best thing. Let's get out of here. Come on everyone; protest is over!" Jim heard one of his pallbearers say as he fell asleep one final time.

2

Cynthia Webber stood in her dimly lit kitchen, looking out the window into the darkness. She watched the snow gently fall in the backyard which was illuminated only by the light at the back door. She cradled a cup of tea with both hands. The snow looked beautiful as it danced in the light. The weather reminded her of her son's second birthday. That day, it had been snowing for only about an hour when Jason, knowing how much his in-laws disliked winter driving, offered to give them a ride so they could enjoy their grandson's birthday, despite the weather.

Jason never returned home. Cynthia was told that a vehicle in oncoming traffic hit an icy patch and crossed the centreline. Jason was killed instantly.

"Mommy," Luke called to Cynthia from the next room. Cynthia put her mug of tea down next to the kitchen sink.

"Coming, baby." Cynthia calmly glided into Luke's room, happy to have her melancholy memory of Jason interrupted. She sat down on the edge of Luke's bed.

"I can't sleep," Luke said looking up at Cynthia with wide eyes.

"I'm about to get ready for bed. Do you want to sleep with me in my bed tonight?" Cynthia comforted Luke. Luke nodded. "Okay, give me two minutes," Cynthia said as she headed back to the kitchen to put her mug in the dishwasher. As she flicked the kitchen light off, she looked out the window at the falling snow and thought about Jason. Happy New Year. Sleep well, my love. It had been over two years since she was able to say those words to Jason, but she told him she loved him every night before she went to bed just as she had when he'd been alive.

"Alright, munchkin, come on," Cynthia said as she passed Luke's bedroom. Luke and Cynthia grew closer than ever after Jason died. Cynthia had her parents for support, but they felt so guilty about Jason's death that Cynthia didn't like to bother them too much even though they enjoyed spending time with Luke.

Luke hopped out of bed and followed Cynthia down the hall to her bedroom. When they reached Cynthia's room, Luke noticed her school books on her desk. "Are you studying, Mommy?"

"The books can wait until tomorrow," Cynthia answered. She was studying to take the Common Final Examination (CFE) to become a Chartered Professional Accountant (CPA). Most of her studying was done after Luke went to bed. Luke always came first. Cynthia was fortunate to work at the Calgary office of Darlington & Associates (D&A), an international accounting firm. They were great about giving Cynthia time to study during her regular work days. Without the extra time, Cynthia knew she wouldn't be as far in her career as she was.

Cynthia met Jason when she first started at D&A as an articling student. In an office with over four hundred staff, Cynthia was placed on Jason's audit team during her first year. Jason was so impressed with Cynthia's eye for detail that he requested she be put on his team again and again. Before long, it wasn't just Cynthia's attention to detail Jason was noticing.

Cynthia turned off her desk lamp and checked her iPhone one last time for the night. Luke climbed on Cynthia's bed with such enthusiasm she wondered how long it would take for him to fall asleep.

"Shall we read a book?" she said pointing to the pile of Luke's books on her nightstand. Luke nodded and pointed to his favourite book. He stretched his arms out wide and said, "I love you this much, Mommy." Luke and Cynthia read *Guess How Much I Love You,* and by the time they were done, Cynthia could tell Luke was getting sleepy. She kissed him goodnight and turned off the light.

Ten minutes later Luke was snoring in Cynthia's arms. Cynthia wiggled her way out of the snuggle and tiptoed over to her desk. She picked up her accounting books and her laptop and headed to the living room. She'd gotten used to very little sleep, between staying up late and getting up early to study before Luke woke up, she only got a few hours each night.

Cynthia brewed a fresh cup of strong tea and got herself set up on the floor with her books on the coffee table in front of the TV. Before long, Cynthia was asleep with her head on her books. Suddenly, a loud racket at the door caused Cynthia to jolt awake. She was out of breath, and her heart was racing. She saw the motion light flicker on the porch outside the kitchen door.

After Jason died, Cynthia started stashing unsuspecting "weapons" around her house to help make her feel safe. Turning everyday objects into weapons also kept Luke from asking too many questions. Although she lived in a reasonably safe neighbourhood, she felt it didn't hurt to have some extra protection.

She quietly ran for a baseball bat that she kept stashed in the pantry. Without turning on any lights, she snuck towards the kitchen porch ready for whatever hoodlum was sneaking around outside. As she got closer to the porch, she noticed the recycling bin had toppled over and Snuffy, Luke's cat, was gleefully sniffing around whatever traces of food had been left on the tin cans. Goddamn cat, Cynthia muttered to herself. She took a deep breath as she put the bat down and headed outside to clean up the mess.

3

The sun would soon be rising in the clear prairie sky. Cynthia made herself another cup of tea and sat down on the couch. She felt there were worse things she could be addicted to as she set her mug down and picked up the TV remote. She switched on the TV to see that PPC, D&A's largest client, was back in the news. It was never ending these days, she thought. An environmental expert was giving a speech about all the things that could go wrong during the construction of the Rocky Mountain Pipeline that would fall 25 kilometres to the south of Calgary.

"The pipeline will act as a transportation system for petroleum and natural gas products going from Southern Alberta to the Northern U.S. Because of the construction, hundreds of thousands of birds will lose their habitat. That doesn't even consider what might happen in the event of a spill or leak in the pipeline. There is also the potential for explosions and fires which would affect our natural environment and the lives of our citizens," Dr. Eve Greenwich, environmental scientist from the University of Calgary, droned on.

Cynthia knew first-hand the type of controversy the Rocky Mountain Pipeline was stirring up. Last week she was threatened by over-enthusiastic environmentalists when she crossed their picket line at PPC to meet with PPC's financial controller Jim Dunn regarding PPC's audit plan. As a CPA student, it was a privilege for Cynthia to be taking on the role of audit manager. D&A was extremely short-staffed during this booming time of growth for the city of Calgary. This was Cynthia's chance to prove she was management material and not just the young widow whom many of her colleagues pitied.

Cynthia had proved she knew her stuff during her first two weeks at D&A. She knew she had attracted Jason's attention even though it was unintentional. She was just doing her job. It wasn't her stunning dark hair or magnetic brown eyes, but Jason would later admit to her that it was the way she handled herself that attracted him. He could tell she was nervous and was trying hard not to let it show but it was clear she wasn't afraid of hard work even though she was out of her element at a new job. Jason admired that.

During her first year in the audit department of D&A, Cynthia worked as a regular member of Jason's team. This was nearly unheard of with a staff of over 300 in the department. Newbies, like Cynthia was at the time, were rotated among managers as team members were needed. As soon as the audit tests were completed, newbies were moved to the next file and the next manager. The lowest members on the totem pole, Associates, rarely saw their managers but instead dealt with Senior Associates who were also working on the assigned file.

"Mommy?" Luke spoke quietly from behind the couch where Cynthia sat watching the news. Cynthia quickly grabbed the remote and zapped the TV off. She hated the controversy and violence happening around the world but especially locally and wanted to protect Luke from as much of it as possible.

"What's up, kiddo?"

"Is it time to get up?" Luke asked. Cynthia checked the clock on the kitchen stove and saw that it was already five minutes after six.

"It is, bud. Do you want some cereal for breakfast?" Luke nodded. Cynthia proceeded to get Luke set up with his breakfast, so she could shower and get ready for another day at PPC's offices.

I can't wait until this audit is over with, Cynthia thought as she put her textbooks back on her desk. Auditing is frustrating enough without all the extra controversy. I better catch up on the news after I drop Luke off. If I'm going to be heading into another angry mob today, just to count a bunch of pipes, I might as wll be prepared.

4

Dr. Eve Greenwich slammed down her coffee cup. "Why can't these companies see the danger here? One wrong move and entire habitats will be gone forever!"

"I understand, Ms. Greenwich, but what about the economy? Do you realize our city would be nothing without the oil and gas industry?" Linda Reeves, investigative reporter for S-CAL, Southern Calgary's most prominent news station, couldn't resist expressing her point of view.

"That's *your* opinion, Ms. Reeves. Do you think I care more about the economy than our environment?" Eve seared. "This earth will be destroyed in no time if we keep letting these monster companies have their way."

"But isn't it the government's way?" Linda questioned.

"Who do you think is lining their pockets? Those oil companies pay a fraction of the tax they should and why do you think that is?" Linda could tell this interview wasn't going to end well so, although she disagreed, she decided it was best to end the conversation.

"I've never really thought about it that way," Linda mustered, feeling slightly bullied by the environmental doctor.

"Well, you really . . ." Eve was cut off by her cell phone ringtone. Linda, having been raised by Beach Boys fans, swore it sounded like *Don't Go Near the Water.* "Excuse me please." Eve glanced up at Linda, turned her back and walked down the hallway as if she had something to hide.

"What? How is that even possible?" Linda could hear Eve down the hall. The reporter in her never stopped working an angle, never stopped listening. "No, we can't meet there. Someone might see us. We can't risk it," Eve said at a barely audible level. "Alright, I'll see you tonight." Eve clicked off her phone and whirled around to get back to her meeting with Linda.

"Are we done here?"

"Uh, sure. Emergency?"

"Just my daughter. She's stuck at a friend's house and needs a ride as soon as possible."

Linda snickered to herself, "Yeah right."

"Thank you for your time, Dr. Greenwich." Linda attempted to play nice but Eve was already halfway out the door. What are you up to Dr. Greenwich? Linda had half a mind to follow her and find out but her time was better spent elsewhere for now.

5

Cynthia dropped Luke off at daycare and arrived at the office at her usual 8 a.m. She had already checked in with her Senior Manager, Sam Johnson. As the audit team manager, it was important for Cynthia to keep Sam informed as to how the audit was going especially on days like today when the audit team would be in the field. Unlike the rest of her audit team, Cynthia hated fieldwork. There was always so much pressure to get things done as quickly as possible, and Cynthia felt she couldn't allow herself the time to take a proper lunch break so most afternoons consisted of her conducting audit tests while hoping her fellow team members couldn't hear the obnoxious gurgling coming from her stomach. If she was lucky, she remembered to pack a lunch and could grab a few snacks while she worked.

While she prepared for the day and reviewed her audit notes, Cynthia found a replay of the Eve Greenwich interview she was watching earlier while she was getting ready for work. It sounded like Eve was making a great case why PPC should stop work on the Rocky Mountain Pipeline. Cynthia felt the demonstrators she had come in contact with at PPC's offices were just fearful of the worst-case scenario. David Jerew, Senior Partner at D&A, and the one signing off on PPC's financial statements wouldn't be happy to hear this. David had many oil and gas clients, but PPC was by far his largest. David was proud of the fact that PPC was not only *his* largest client but the firm's largest as well. He certainly used those bragging rights every chance he got. Cynthia didn't see David much. He was usually schmoozing with his clients, taking them to fancy, expensive lunches or off in Toronto at firm mandated meetings.

As Eve Greenwich made her final statement in the case against PPC, Cynthia turned off the interview and folded up her laptop to pack it in her audit bag. She was sure she would see more interviews from Dr. Greenwich. It was almost time to head to PPC's main office on the other side of town. Today was the day the inventory count had to be finished if the audit was going to stay on schedule (as if that was an option). David Jerew did not put up with late audits. Cynthia had been elected to drive to PPC, but her audit team was nowhere to be found.

Like Cynthia, Ben Wilson and Ryan Devereau were preparing to take the CPA final examination. Cynthia thought maybe they were in the meeting room studying while they were waiting for her to get to the office but that didn't sound like them. More than likely she would find them shootin' the shit over their third cup of coffee. Both Ben and Ryan had a party animal reputation and last night was New Year's Eve after all. Cynthia still couldn't believe they were all working today, but then again, hardly anyone took time off in this city—even for the holidays.

Cynthia had no idea how Ben and Ryan did as well as they had so far in the CPA program. Cynthia checked the meeting room anyway. It was dark. She took another pass by Ryan's and Ben's cubicles. Thankfully they worked side by side. What a mess. There were old lunch wrappers on the desks, books all over the floor, and wrinkled clothes on their chairs. Two peas in a pod, she thought.

As Cynthia rounded the bend to the reception area, she saw Sheryl, the 41st-floor office manager.

"Have you seen Ben or Ryan this morning?"

"Sorry dear, not yet," Sheryl replied nonchalantly.

"Thanks. Hopefully I'll be back this afternoon if I can get this count finished," Cynthia checked in with Sheryl.

"Good luck." Sheryl waved at the back of Cynthia's head as she got into the elevator.

Cynthia rode the 41 floors down to the parkade, getting more irritated as the elevator hummed along. By the time she got to her car, she had gone from angry to fuming, but she knew she had the 45-minute drive to PPC to calm down. She was hoping Ben and Ryan just misunderstood and thought they were supposed to meet her at PPC, not downtown at D&A's office. She felt a huge burden settling on her shoulders as she tried to come up with a game plan to complete the inventory count by herself and still keep the audit on schedule so she wouldn't have to deal with the wrath of David Jerew.

6

Ben and Ryan owe me for covering for their sorry asses. They're probably still drunk. Rang in the new year at O'Leary's last night, I bet. I'm so glad to be done with my twenties. Inventory needs to be confirmed today, and I'm not going to risk my promotion by not getting it done. This sure is the strangest inventory count I've done in my auditing career. Getting in and out of the yard before the pipe is pulled for the day's projects is going to be key.

Cynthia pulled into the parking lot at PPC and felt a sense of relief. Not because she saw Ben or Ryan but because of what she didn't see. A picket line. One less thing to deal with this morning. The brilliant, clear blue sky seemed to be smiling at this thought too. Julie Mann, Assistant Controller, was already hard at work. Seems like she's covering for a sorry ass too, Cynthia thought. Jim Dunn, Controller, had been AWOL since yesterday. Nobody at PPC had seen or heard from him which was unusual because he was always at the office during audit season and he told Cynthia he'd be around every day during her fieldwork.

"Morning, Julie."

"Hi, Cynthia. You headed back to the yard again?"

"You bet. Need to finish counting those pipes before the trucks start loading."

"What happened to Ben and Ryan?"

"Oh, I'm sure they'll turn up eventually. Any word from Jim?"

"Nope."

"Well, you seem to have things under control. I better get to it. See you later."

Next to the office was the yard where PPC housed all the pipe they needed to construct their pipelines as well as their equipment. Today the yard looked like it was home to a swarm of gargantuan mutant bees. There were pipes with diameters ranging from 2 to 60 inches, and they were stacked in such a way they looked like gigantic honeycombs. Thankfully, they were stacked by size which made counting them a lot easier. Cynthia realized she sure didn't need the help of a couple of hung-over frat boys.

It was shaping up to be a beautiful day except for a slightly foul smell in the yard. There was a by-product plant over on Southview. When the wind kicked up, it could get pretty nasty in the yard, and the wind was coming from that direction today thanks to one of Calgary's famous Chinooks. Cynthia tried to ignore the smell by reminding herself she was happy to have some time to enjoy the yard before everyone started their day and the forklifts started stirring up the dust.

D&A had recently purchased some tablets for the audit department that were designed especially for inventory counts to make the process more efficient. No need to take notes then enter them into a laptop later. Cynthia entered the pipe count directly into her tablet which already had all the pipe sizes listed. All she had to do was fill in the blanks.

Cynthia noticed a shoe in the yard. What in the world?

"Ben? Ryan? Is this your idea of a joke? Get your butts out here and help me finish this count!" Cynthia looked towards the main office, but all she saw through the window was Julie busy at her computer. She decided she better go check it out.

As Cynthia got closer to the shoe, she could see it was a brown Gucci and large enough to be a man's. Ben and Ryan definitely didn't wear Gucci. Not only was it weird for a shoe to be in the middle of the yard, but as best as Cynthia could tell, there was only one. Cynthia decided to take it inside and see if anyone knew who it belonged to, but first, she wanted to finish the row of 24-inch pipe so she didn't have to break in the middle of a section. The section of 24-inch pipes was eight pipes high by fourteen pipes long—one-hundred and twelve of those babies.

Cynthia headed towards the office to get the beautiful, Gucci shoe back inside where it belonged. She couldn't help but laugh at her own shoes as she walked back to the office. After spending a couple of hours counting pipe yesterday morning, Cynthia decided her usual heels didn't belong in the yard, and she opted for a more comfortable pair of loafers that didn't really match her outfit. The blisters on her feet were grateful for the change.

As she walked to the end of the row, towards the office, the pipe diameters got larger. Cynthia passed a section that looked to be about three-feet wide. Cynthia saw a white sedan pull into the parking lot. Maybe Jim had decided to come to work today after all. Cynthia hurried inside to give the shoe to Julie before she and Gordon James, PPC CFO, had their morning meeting.

"Julie. Does this shoe look familiar? It's a Gucci."

"Yeah, that's Jim's. Where did you find it?"

"Over by the 24-inch pipes. Only the left foot. Thought someone might be missing it."

Julie and Cynthia shared a couple of strange looks as Gord entered the office. Julie and Gord engaged in small talk as Cynthia headed back to the yard. She needed to hurry if she was going to get the rest of the pipe counted before the crews started loading up for the day.

Cynthia was heading back to where she left off when she noticed one of the 36-inch pipes looked like it had something in it. Maybe it was the matching shoe? Cynthia decided to check it out. As she got closer to the pipe, Cynthia realized it was a shoe alright, but it was attached to a body.

7

"Oh my God! Jim! Jim, can you hear me? Help! Help! Call 9-1-1!" Cynthia screamed as loud as she could from the yard. Jim smelled awful, like meat that had been left out far too long on a blistering hot day. The fumes were so strong Cynthia couldn't help retching as she tried to see inside the pipe. At one point she lurched close enough to the body to see there was something sparkling just inside Jim's collar. She noticed his flesh had a bluish tint to it. This can't be a good sign, she thought. Why isn't anyone coming to help me? Damn it!

Cynthia started running towards the office trying not to pass out or vomit on the way.

"Julie, call 9-1-1!" she yelled as loudly as she could, but then she remembered the office glass was soundproof so the accountants could still work and not be bothered by the equipment noise in the yard. Cynthia flung the door open, out of breath, "Call 9-1-1. I think it's Jim!" she said in a frantic panic.

"What?!" Julie picked up the phone and dialed 9-1-1. Gord swiveled around in his fancy chair to see what the commotion was about. He could see Cynthia was physically affected by what she found in the pipe.

"What do you mean it's Jim and why do we need to call 9-1-1?" Gord asked confused.

"The pipe, the pipe, Jim's in the pipe," Cynthia shrieked, still shocked from what she'd seen. "Third row . . . gasp . . . down in the first section of . . . gasp . . . 36-inch."

"Okay, try to breathe, calm down. Are you sure it's Jim?" Gord asked.

"Yes, I'm sure. He's wearing the other Gucci and I got a lot closer than I would have liked," Cynthia said as she tried to calm herself down. It wouldn't look good to break down in front of the CFO, she thought, but if she didn't find a chair fast, she was going to pass out. Luckily she found one in front of Julie's desk. Julie was still on the line with 9-1-1. Cynthia felt like her face was on fire. Although she was hot and felt like she was sweating, her face was as white as the paper in the printer on Julie's desk.

In and out, in and out, was all Cynthia kept thinking to herself. That and ...why? Why was Jim in that pipe and how did he get there? How long had he been there? It had only been a few weeks since Cynthia met with Jim to discuss the initial audit plan. This must be a nightmare. It can't be real!

The blaring siren of the ambulance jolted Cynthia from her thoughts back to reality. She could see the ambulance through the office window and a little beyond that she saw a police car. She took another deep breath. Wow. The ambulance parked right outside the front doors, and two emergency medical technicians jumped out and ran inside.

"They're here now," Julie said hanging up the phone while Gord directed the men outside to the pipe where Jim's body lay.

Cynthia was in a complete daze still sitting in the chair in front of Julie's desk. She couldn't get the smell of Jim's body out of her nose and the sight of his blue skin banished from her mind. She didn't doubt Jim was dead and had been for quite some time. She looked up and out the office window slowly, hoping that by some magical chance Jim was still alive and she would see him being strapped to a stretcher. No such luck. Gord and one of the EMT's were standing in front of the pipe where Jim's body lay hidden from view. The other EMT was climbing out of the pipe shaking his head.

Gord turned and jogged back to the office while the EMT's waited to be questioned by the police. Cynthia found it odd that Gord didn't look any different than he did any other day. He didn't seem surprised by the morning's events. It seemed like this was a normal day for him. Business as usual. Two police officers entered through the front doors as Gord came from the yard door to the side. Cynthia turned to face the officers. She knew since she was the one who had discovered the body, they were going to need a statement from her.

"Who found the body?" the younger officer probed.

"I . . ." Cynthia started to speak but was cut off.

"I did," said Gord.

"But . . ." Cynthia stammered. What is going on? What is Gord doing? Julie and Cynthia looked at each other with confusion in their eyes. Julie shrugged and lifted her eyebrows. Not knowing what else to do, Cynthia looked down at the carpeted floor and listened in, hoping for a clue as to why Gord was claiming this gruesome discovery as his own.

8

The door swung open, and Ben and Ryan cautiously crossed the office threshold.

"It's about bloody time you two showed up!" Cynthia couldn't control her emotions anymore. She was angry at Ben and Ryan for being late and leaving her to count inventory on her own, and she was angry she discovered Jim's body instead of one of them. Both Ben and Ryan stopped dead in their tracks, not expecting to walk into the commotion they'd happened upon.

"What's going on?" Ryan asked sheepishly.

"What's going on?!" Cynthia tried not to screech but the incredulousness of the last hour had gotten the better of her. Her face was on fire, and her cheeks were numb like they had tiny needles covering them like pincushions. She took a deep breath trying to figure out how she was going to explain what had gone on in the last hour. All she could think to say was, "You're an hour late, that's what's going on." Then the tears came. Finally.

"Could one of you take Cynthia home?" Julie jumped to Cynthia's rescue. "You guys will have to come back tomorrow. We're closing the office for the day in light of this morning's events."

"But we still don't know what's going on," Ryan insisted. Julie motioned for Ben and Ryan to step into Jim's office. Ironic. They didn't close the door, so Cynthia could hear every word they exchanged. Julie told Ben and Ryan how Cynthia had discovered Jim's body an hour or so ago and how she'd been just about catatonic since then.

"Her shouting at you was the first thing I've heard her say since everything happened. She needs to get some rest or maybe even get checked out at the hospital. The police told us it's common for people to go into shock after seeing something like that."

"Did you see him?" Ben asked.

"No. I'm not even sure if Gord saw him when he went out in the yard to show the EMTs where he was."

"He was in the yard?"

"Yeah, in one of the three-foot pipes."

"Jesus! Do you know what happened?"

"The police are treating it like murder right now."

"Shit, we better get back to the office and let Sam know this audit isn't going to be done anytime soon. David is *not* going to like this."

"Can you take Cynthia to the hospital?"

"Of course, the office can wait." Cynthia heard Ryan and Ben exit Jim's office with Julie close behind them. She suddenly realized she didn't even know where her tablet and laptop were. She guessed she must have dropped them when she was running to the office. She was about to ask if anyone had seen them when she noticed Ryan packing her laptop bag for her. Ben offered Cynthia his hand to stand, but she declined and told him, in a snarky tone, that she was fine. She instantly regretted it.

"I'm sorry, it's just . . ."

"We know," Ben cut her off. "Don't worry about it." He gently patted Cynthia's shoulder. As she got up to leave, she noticed Julie's phone had started ringing non-stop. The high call volume was unusual for January 1st, a day most people would take off to relax. Stakeholders and reporters no doubt. News like this travelled fast in Calgary. It wasn't every day a top accountant at one of the city's largest pipeline companies was found dead and stuffed inside a pipe. Cynthia still couldn't believe it. She hoped she would wake up from this horrible nightmare any minute.

9

Detective Randy Bain of the Calgary Police Department took a sip of his now cold coffee and placed it on the table in front of him, trying not to grimace as he swallowed the vile brew. "You're free to go, Mr. James. Someone will contact you if we have further questions. Is there someone in your office you can talk to? A professional counsellor maybe? Discovering a body can be quite traumatic. We do have an outreach worker here if you need someone to talk to. Here's her card."

"Thank you, Detective." Gord accepted the card and placed it in his shirt pocket. He shook Randy's hand as he rose from the table and left the interrogation room. As he hurried down the hall, he heard his cell phone pinging in his pants pocket. What now? He glanced at the screen as he silenced the ringer.

Blue Hyundai. 3rd and 51st. In the alley. ASAP!

WTF? was his reply.

Just get here.

By this time, Gord was already out the door of the police station. Jesus, this better be good. He hurried down the concrete steps almost skipping a step and losing his balance as he went. The police station was close to downtown in a high traffic area, so he opted to hoof it to the meeting spot. He kept his phone in his hand as he went.

Gord couldn't help but notice the change of scenery as he got further away from downtown. Not the landscape, but the people. He was on the east side of town now. The area of town where people who had nowhere else to go, went to live.

"Spare some change?" he heard a man call out as he walked past. Gord kept going as if he hadn't heard him. He was glad he only had a few blocks to go. It was a chilly winter day, but the stress of the events at PPC, along with the cryptic text was causing his blood to boil. He removed his sports coat and flung it over his shoulder as he continued at a speed-walkers pace.

From the street, Gord couldn't see his rendezvous car, but as soon as he turned down the alley, it was there. He picked up the pace and jumped in the front passenger seat.

"What the hell, Eve? This is a little different from our usual spot, don't you think?"

"We can't risk being seen," Eve replied in a cold tone as if she was annoyed at Gord for questioning her. "Especially now. It's not about sex this time."

"What do you mean?"

"Jim. The police are treating his death like murder, aren't they?"

"How do you know about that?"

"It doesn't matter."

"Oh, come on, Eve, how can you say it doesn't matter? And what does Jim's death have to do with us?" Gord tried to convince her, but he knew she was right. If anyone found out they'd been having an affair, it would draw all kinds of unwanted attention, not only to the both of them but also to their respective employers. Public appearance was everything in a town with so much controversy.

"There was supposed to be a public protest at PPC today to kick off the new year, but when the demonstrators arrived and found the place looking like a ghost town, they retreated. One of my teaching assistants, April, is friends with Julie, so I asked her to find out what was going on. Julie didn't want to say anything but April could tell she wanted to get something off her chest. We can't be seen together."

"Okay, well where do you want to go?" Gord leaned close to Eve and tried to kiss her neck.

"I told you, it's not about sex today. I forgot how young you really are."

"Come on, Eve, you've never cared that I'm half your age."

"Well, I have a husband and kids to worry about. Not to mention the career that I've worked the last twenty years to build."

"What are you saying?"

"It's over."

"Come on, Eve. You can't really mean that. We've got a good thing going. You can't just end it like that."

"I can, and I am. Get out, Gord!"

Gord got out and barely slammed the door before Eve peeled out of the alleyway in reverse and yanked the Hyundai out onto the road narrowly missing oncoming traffic. Whose car is that anyway? Gord thought as he watched the taillights disappear.

10

As the blue Hyundai sped down the road towards the on-ramp for the northbound highway, Eve's eyes stung, and her cheeks felt like they had been slapped hard. She was angry about so many things today. Having an affair, having a career that kept her so busy, and having to fight to be heard on the environmental front. Most of all, she was angry with herself for getting so attached to a young, charismatic businessman half her age and on the opposite side of the environmental fight. They were both in the prime of their careers, but Eve was twenty-five years older than Gord. This made her angry too. She wanted to cry but wouldn't allow herself.

Eve's drive back to the university took longer than she would have liked. Rush hour was starting, and the extra vehicles on the highway were beginning to make things less maneuverable. While Eve was stuck in a slow-moving lane, she looked out across the fields to her right. She could vaguely make out the PPC offices. There appeared to be a news van there. Ghost town no more. Eve thought she'd better tune into the news later and find out what the real story was.

The massive parking lot at the University of Calgary was packed. Eve started looking for April's parking spot. She parked the Hyundai and quickly headed for the environmental sciences building. Her meeting with Gord had set her back about an hour, and she needed to make that time up as quickly as possible.

April was in her office next to Eve's. It appeared as though she had been grading papers and Eve couldn't help but notice how focused April was on her laptop. She could hear Linda Reeves' voice projecting from the laptop but couldn't hear what she was saying.

"Thanks love," Eve said to April as she put April's Hyundai keys down on the desk.

"No problem. Did you make it to your daughter's recital in time?"

"Oh, yeah, I did. Thanks! I would never have made it in time by train." Eve had already forgotten about the little white lie she told April when she asked to borrow her car at the last minute. Eve liked April. She was a hard worker and one of the brightest teaching assistants Eve had. She was just as passionate about the environment as Eve, and Eve hoped she would be able to convince April to stay on at the university once she had completed her doctorate degree. Eve hated lying to April, but it was for the best.

11

Cynthia woke up at the hospital and quickly realized from the stark surroundings where she was. Her mouth was dry, and her head was pounding. Her mom, Gayle, was standing at the foot of her bed. She saw that Cynthia was about to talk but beat her to it.

"Ben called me. He told me something happened at work and that he needed to go back to the office, but he and Ryan didn't want to leave you alone at the hospital. I've already talked to the doctor. She said you're in shock, but it's just a mild case. You'll feel better after a good rest."

"Okay, do I need to wait for the doctor?" At this point, all Cynthia wanted to do was go home, lie down in her comfy bed, and try to stop thinking about Jim's body and why Gord had said he found it. The doctor must have read Cynthia's mind. She walked over to Cynthia's bed looking at some notes on a clipboard.

"You're free to go." She looked at Cynthia and gave her a reassuring smile.

"Thank you." Cynthia breathed a sigh of relief.

Gayle and Cynthia made their way through the maze of people and hospital beds. There certainly wasn't a lack of activity around there. They stopped at the reception desk to sign required paperwork and then they were on their way.

Cynthia wasn't looking forward to the drive to home. Gayle told her she'd cleared her day to make sure she was okay. "Doctor's orders, you know." There was no arguing with Gayle.

Other than feeling like she'd been up for a week, Cynthia felt fine, but Gayle insisted on picking up Cynthia's dad, Bob, on the way so he could stay with Cynthia while Gayle went to get Luke from daycare.

The ride to get Bob was quiet. Although Cynthia didn't outwardly blame her parents for Jason's accident over two years ago, she felt like she wasn't herself around them. She couldn't help but think Jason would still be alive had he not gone to pick them up that day. Cynthia knew they thought it too. The elephant in the room. They hardly ever talked about Jason anymore because of it. Cynthia was determined to keep Jason's memory alive. Just not around her parents.

Cynthia was relieved when Gayle finally pulled into the driveway. She could always count on her dad for some ridiculous knee-slap joke. Cynthia felt like her dad still thought of her as his awkward little ten-year-old girl with pigtails. Today though, he looked at Cynthia differently.

"Everything alright?" Bob asks, getting into the back seat behind Cynthia.

"I'm fine. Are you sure you want to sit in the back? It feels strange sitting in the front while you sit back there." Bob wasn't a tall man, but Cynthia knew he didn't like to feel cramped.

"I'm alright, Cyndi. Let's go, Gayle. You know, that Ben boy sure had us worried when he called to tell us you were in the hospital. He didn't give us any details though, what's going on?"

Ignoring the question Cynthia replied, "Ben's hardly a boy, Dad. He's 27-years-old."

"You're his boss, so that makes him a boy to me." To this Cynthia laughs a bit for the first time all day.

"I'm not his boss; I'm just the audit manager. It's up to me to make sure this audit gets done on time, so we can all avoid David's wrath." Cynthia rolled her eyes, thinking about David Jerew. "Ben and Ryan are part of my team. We also have a Senior Manager who is counting on us not to piss David off."

"Ooooh, the wrath of David." Cynthia couldn't see Bob, but she felt like he gestured towards the sky as if David had some sort of all-knowing power.

"He's worked hard to get to the level he's at in his career, Dad. Can you blame him for holding his staff up to certain standards?"

"Sure, but he doesn't have to treat his staff so badly. I remember you talking about him throwing temper tantrums and acting like a child. You can have standards and still be professional about it." Bob looked out the window. "Hey, you never answered my question. Why were you in the hospital? I didn't realize a bean counter's work was so dangerous."

"Oh, Dad, if only you knew. I'm sure mom will fill you in. I just want to lay down right now."

12

Cynthia woke to the smell of her mom's lasagna—her favourite. She felt like she had slept right through to the next day, but she hadn't, it was still Monday. Cynthia got out of bed, put on her slippers and a sweater, and groggily staggered towards her kitchen. She was expecting to see her parents and Luke, but only her dad was home.

"There she is. How are you feeling?" Bob stood up from where he was watching TV.

"Better. Where's Mom?'

"She just went to get Luke. She'll be back soon. Oh, your friend Linda called."

"Oh shoot! I better check my cell. Linda's the only one who ever calls the house. She might be the only one who has the number, besides you guys. Thanks, Dad. Excuse me for a minute."

"Of course, kiddo."

Cynthia went to her room to find her cell phone. Five missed calls and four messages. A sigh escaped Cynthia's lips as she scanned the call display. Three calls from the office, one from Linda, and a number she didn't recognize. So much for getting lots of rest, Cynthia thought as she dialed her voicemail.

"Hi, Cynthia. This is Detective Randy Bain of the Calgary police. I understand you were at Prairie Pipeline Company when the body of Jim Dunn was discovered. I'd like to ask you a few questions. Please call me back at 905-555-9000." Cynthia saved the message as a reminder to call the detective later.

"I'm really sorry, Cynthia. It's Sam. David is on my ass about PPC. We need to press on according to schedule. I'm stuck working the McGregor Inc. audit. I know it's asking a lot of you, but I have faith in you, and you *will* be rewarded come promotion time."

"Cynthia, just so you know, it's business as usual at PPC. I expect this audit to finish on time and you've got some catching up to do now. Prove you're management material and get it done." Yes, David. Cynthia's eyes rolled as she deleted David's message.

"Hey! It's Ben. Just got the word from Sam that things are going ahead as planned. Ryan and I will finish the inventory count first thing in the morning and meet you at the office afterward. Save you the trip out to PPC and make up for being late today. And, I hope you're feeling okay." Something about the tone of Ben's voice assured Cynthia he was serious about making up for being late this morning. She was relieved she wouldn't have to go to PPC in the morning.

Cynthia called Detective Bain and set up an appointment to meet with him the day after tomorrow. She dialed Linda's number. It barely rang before she heard her best friend's voice.

"Oh my god, Cyn! Are you okay? What the hell?"

Cynthia chuckled to herself as she listened to Linda. After all her years as an investigative reporter, Cynthia thought there wasn't anything that would surprise Linda.

"I'm fine. You know, just another day at the office." Cynthia chuckled out loud this time.

"Ah, right, because everybody finds bodies at work."

"Actually, do you mind if we talk about it later? The thought still makes me a little queasy. I'm surprised you heard about it so quickly."

"Of course, but I want all the details when you're feeling better. PPC is big money in this city, and they're already under such close watch by the environmentalists. Anything that happens out there gets to the newsroom pretty fast."

"So, will this be off the record?"

"You know it's always off the record with you. You know you're the only person that applies to."

"And you're the only reporter I actually believe when you say that. Mom's making lasagna if you want to stop by."

"Ahh, you're killing me! I'm going to have to work through dinner tonight with this crazy story. I'll take a rain check though."

"You got it. Later, my friend."

"You better get some rest."

"Ha, right! David doesn't know the meaning of the word."

"Screw him!"

"Screw him means I screw my promotion and my raise!"

"It's only money, Cyn."

"Yeah, yeah. Talk soon."

As Cynthia clicked her phone off, she heard her dad in the other room. "Come on, you bastard!" She ran out to her living room to see what was going on.

13

"**Dad?! Oh, geez!** I should have known you were watching hockey. You scared me for a minute there. I must be on edge from this morning still."

"You'll feel better once you get some of that lasagna in you."

"That's the truth. Mom's lasagna has seen me through some pretty tough times." As the words rolled out of Cynthia's tongue, she saw Luke and Gayle pull up in the driveway. She ran out the door to get a hug from her favourite little man, relieved that now Luke was home there wouldn't be much talk about dead bodies and PPC.

It was nice to enjoy a family meal together again. It didn't happen often enough since Jason died. Luke also didn't spend near enough time with his grandparents. After Jason died, Cynthia became fearful to leave Luke with her parents. It wasn't that she felt like he would be ill-cared for. Quite the opposite, actually. Her parents were very loving grandparents, but Cynthia didn't like Luke leaving her side unless she was working. She was afraid she would lose him too. As ridiculous as she knew this was, it caused her great anxiety to leave Luke with her parents.

"Do you want one of us to spend the night to make sure you're okay?" Gayle offered.

"It's alright, Mom. I'll be fine. I've got my little man to take care of me." Gayle's expression became irritated as she walked over to Cynthia and leaned in close so Luke couldn't hear what she was about to say.

"He's four years old, dear. You can't be saying things like that. It's a lot of responsibility for someone so young."

"Mom, I . . ." Cynthia cut herself off knowing what she wanted to say would just lead to an argument. An argument she didn't have the energy for right now. She took a deep breath. "I know. Thank you for dinner. It was a relief not to have to cook, and you know how much I love your lasagna."

"Anytime, dear." And with that, Cynthia's parents left for the night.

Cynthia started running a bath for Luke but then, realising how late it was, decided she would have the bath after Luke was sleeping. She stopped the water with the tub partially full and turned to Luke. "Alright, my friend, the good news is, you get to skip your bath tonight. The bad news is it's time for bed." Luke protested a little but agreed to sleep in Cynthia's bed again. Cynthia read him a story then headed next door to the bathroom to finish filling the tub and have a relaxing soak. She couldn't keep her mind from wandering back to the image of Jim in that pipe. Why would anyone kill Jim? He seemed like such a hardworking, nice guy.

14

Outside the environmental sciences building at the University of Calgary, David leaned against a wall sucking on a cigarette. In jeans and a black hoody, he blended in with the students on campus even though he was in his late fifties. Sunglasses covered his eyes for added anonymity. There was a restraining order against him to stay away from the campus, but it had been years since he paid attention to it. Although usually from the comfort of his Escalade, he'd been staking out the environmental sciences building for quite some time. David saw the young woman he was waiting for, walking towards him with a man he'd seen on the news plenty of times protesting against PPC and their pipeline construction. His hands balled into fists in his pockets and he angled his body away from them as they approached.

"It's at PPC? Are you sure?" David heard the man say to the woman.

"Yes! I felt it fall out of my ear. I was hoping you might have seen it and picked it up."

"Not exactly something I would notice." The couple continued walking and David, intent on hearing the rest of their conversation, followed as closely as he could without being noticed.

"Did you see the news? He died."

"The guy from PPC? Oh my god! No, I didn't see that.

You didn't call 9-1-1, did you?" The man looked down at the ground before answering.

"Uh…"

"What?! You just left him there to die? You promised you would call!"

"I'm sorry, I didn't think it was that bad. We put him in a pipe. We thought he would be okay in there."

"This is bad. This is really bad. I killed a man! Shit! I need to go to the police."

"Are you crazy? You'll be arrested for murder."

"It was an accident. I'm sure if I explain everything, they'll understand."

"You're talking about a man's life. What they'll understand is that he's no longer breathing because you killed him."

"I need to find that earring!"

"You can't go to PPC now. That place will be swarming with cops."

"Why should I listen to you? I can't believe you would leave an injured man to die." The woman turned around and stormed off back the way she came, towards David.

"I told you, I didn't know he was going to die." The man pleaded to the back of her head but didn't try to follow.

David veered off the path to avoid recognition. He knew if she saw him, she'd be hysterical over his breaking the restraining order she'd filed so many years ago. He looked back in the scientist's direction and cursed under his breath.

"No good activist!" He knew that man wasn't going to do anything to help find the earring, but he had an idea how he could help instead.

15

"Mommy?" Luke quietly whispered, tapping Cynthia on the arm. When Cynthia finally woke up, she regrettably noticed it was time to get ready for work. Her head was throbbing, and she felt a little sick to her stomach.

"Hi, buddy," Cynthia whispered to Luke. "You know what? We need to get ready really fast this morning, okay?"

"Why?" Luke asked.

"I've got a lot of work to do today, but I'm going to stop by and spend my lunch break with you."

"Yay! Can we have peanut butter sandwiches?"

"Not today, little man. You know we can't bring peanut butter to the daycare. We'll have peanut butter soon though. Go get dressed, and I'll get your breakfast ready."

Cynthia quickly put on a skirt and blouse and picked out some pretty heels making sure to choose a comfortable pair. Heels always gave her a little boost when she didn't feel like working and today was one of those days. She was trying hard not to think about everything she needed to get done. At least she didn't have to worry about running into David. He was almost never in the office, and when he was, he was always busy with his door closed.

Luke and Cynthia were ready for their commute in record time. Cynthia was sure she was forgetting something, but after checking Luke's backpack three times, she knew Luke had everything he would need at daycare, and that was the most important thing. The drive to the office was uneventful. Because they had gotten ready so quickly, the morning rush-hour traffic wasn't too heavy yet. Cynthia preferred to drive to work so she didn't have to take Luke on the 90-minute bus ride. The drive from her place to downtown was only half that time, and she and Luke talked or listened to the radio. Luke loved music.

"You're here early," Luke's caregiver Rachel beamed at Luke. Cynthia always felt confident leaving Luke for the day, and because the daycare was just for employees of D&A, they were understanding when she stopped by to check-in on Luke at random times throughout the day.

"Alright, sweetie, I'll see you later." Cynthia gave Luke a big kiss and hug and headed upstairs to start working on a game plan to finish the audit in time.

Cynthia was at her desk almost an hour earlier than usual. She liked how quiet the office was at this time of the morning. Having spent many years in a cubicle, Cynthia was used to the noise from staff coming and going and working on both sides of her, but she still relished the quiet. It was her prime time. She organized her thoughts and banged out a plan to get the audit finished on time. It would mean some long hours at the office to make up for yesterday, but it was doable. She got to work on PPC's file, skipping the inventory section for now but otherwise picking up where she left off.

Just before lunch, Cynthia felt a tap on her shoulder which nearly had her jumping out of her seat. It was Ryan. Cynthia smiled and took her earbuds out as she grabbed towards her heart.

"Sorry," Ryan said, trying not to smirk. "I wanted to let you know the inventory count is done and logged into the system. You should see it on the network now."

"Perfect, thank you so much. I wasn't looking forward to being at PPC today."

"We thought that might be the case. Julie asked about you. She and Gord seem to be managing pretty well considering. A news van got there just as we were leaving."

"I'm sure that's going to be non-stop until they figure out what happened. Did you and Ben give your statements already?"

"Yes, there wasn't much for us to say since we missed all the excitement. Detective Bain's pretty cool." Ryan seemed overly excited to have met a detective, and Cynthia couldn't help but laugh at Ryan's comment.

"Okay, thanks for the update on the audit. Sam and I are meeting after lunch to go over the new game plan. Let's meet with Ben after that and figure out how to make this happen."

"You got it. I'll let him know," Ryan agreed as he turned and headed back to his desk.

Cynthia took a quick break to have lunch with Luke at daycare then was back to the 41st floor for her meeting with Sam. He liked the new plan and felt comfortable the audit would still finish on time and most of all, keep David happy.

When Cynthia checked her watch again, it was already past six. She was starting to get tired, and her thoughts were certainly not as clear as they had been when her workday started almost eleven hours ago. Luke's daycare would be closing soon.

It was a productive day. Cynthia was impressed with Ben and Ryan's efforts, and how quickly they were able to finish the inventory count and get back to the office to help her with the remaining working papers and audit checklists that needed to be completed. As she packed her bag, she noticed there was a message on her cell phone.

"Hi, Cynthia. This is the Calgary police department calling to remind you of your meeting with Detective Randy Bain at 11 o'clock tomorrow morning. If you cannot attend this meeting, please call us to reschedule." Thankfully, Cynthia did remember, and she was looking forward to talking with Detective Bain. She informed Sheryl she would be out of the office for a couple of hours to attend the meeting. Cynthia exhaled long and slow, allowing for a mini-pause before heading to pick up Luke.

16

After a long day like today, Cynthia was glad Luke's daycare was just a short elevator ride away. This would be the third time she stopped at the 21st floor today. As the elevator dinged and its doors opened, Cynthia thought she saw the back of David's head. That's weird, what's he doing here? He doesn't have any kids. As she got closer to the art tables, Cynthia realized she was right, and David was sitting, drawing with Luke.

"Hi David," Cynthia said, puzzled. "What are you doing here?"

"Mommy!!" Luke ran to Cynthia and jumped into her arms.

"I just thought I'd stop in to make sure the company-recommended daycare was topnotch. How long have you been bringing Luke here?"

"Almost a year now," Cynthia replied, believing David's story. "It's a wonderful place. Luke loves it, and they're always so great when I visit him on my lunch breaks."

"Have a seat, Cynthia," David motioned for Cynthia to sit next to him on the rectangular cushioned bench which barely had room for one adult. Cynthia was hesitant, but David was a senior partner, and with her review coming up, she certainly didn't want to piss him off. Cynthia sat down with Luke still in her arms.

"Luke, why don't you collect your things? I want to talk to your mom for a minute." Luke stared at David, not sure what to do next. Even though Luke was only four, he had become Cynthia's little protector after Jason died.

"It's okay, sweetie, go get your backpack. I'll be right here with Mr. Jerew." Comforted by Cynthia's words, Luke tootled off to where the daycare workers had been playing with the other children.

There was an awkward silence between Cynthia and David.

"I heard you found Jim Dunn's body. That must have been quite the shock for you."

"Yes," Cynthia replied, surprised by David's concern.

"Have you talked to the police yet?" David pried.

"I'm going to meet with the detective tomorrow. I noticed something on the body." Cynthia thought about the small sparkle she saw near Jim's collar.

"Oh, really? What was that?"

"I'm not sure. A crystal maybe?" Cynthia's voice faltered as she became uncomfortable with David's piercing stare.

Leaning in close and placing his hand on her inner thigh, David whispered in her ear, "If you tell the detective about that earring, you're done." As he tightened his grip with an aggressive squeeze, he spat his words angrily in Cynthia's ear, "I'm serious. Your career, your family, everything you've worked for will be gone forever."

David twisted his hand and pinched Cynthia's thigh as he got up and silently scuttled to the elevator before any of the daycare workers saw the intensity with which he was talking to her. Cynthia's breath caught in her chest. An earring, yes, that's what it was, but how did David know that? She tried hard to swallow her tears, so Luke wouldn't suspect anything. She took a deep breath before standing as Luke came back with Rachel, Little Seedling's administrator.

"Did you have a nice visit with your brother?" Rachel asked Cynthia.

Cynthia was confused, "My brother?"

"Yes, David. He said he was your brother."

"Oh, y-yes, that's right," Cynthia, still trying to catch her breath, wasn't sure how to handle this new information. She pulled Rachel aside, "Rachel, could you make sure you call me if David comes back to see Luke, please? I just don't trust him, and I don't want him visiting Luke without me. Luke is definitely not to leave here with him EVER!"

"Of course, Cynthia, no problem. We don't have him listed on Luke's family contact sheet so there's no way we would let Luke leave with him."

"Please leave him *off* that list. Come on, sweetie, let's go home and make some dinner," Cynthia said, calling Luke over. "Thank you, Rachel, you always take such good care of Luke."

"Of course, Cynthia, that's my job."

As Cynthia and Luke got into the elevator, Cynthia swore she could smell the unforgettable mix of David's obnoxious cologne and cigarette smoke. Disgusting.

On the ride down, the elevator dinged as half a dozen people got on at the sixth floor. Cynthia held Luke's hand tightly, still shaking from her encounter with David. She remembered her interview with Detective Bain tomorrow, and she wasn't sure how she was going to handle it given David's threat. She took a deep breath in through her nose and out through her mouth. You'll figure it out Cyndi, you always do.

As the elevator doors opened into the parking garage, Cynthia noticed it was a little less busy than it usually was this time of night. Still feeling uneasy, she pressed the unlock button on her key and watched as the lights to her red Ford Focus flashed, signalling the vehicle was unlocked. She popped the trunk and tossed in her purse and Luke's backpack. After safely securing Luke in his car seat, Cynthia plopped herself down in the driver's seat and fastened her seatbelt as she started the car.

Putting the car in reverse and glancing over her left shoulder a pang of fear raced through her as she saw David waiting in his black Escalade. Cynthia pretended not to see him. She didn't want to alarm Luke, but she also hoped it was just a coincidence David was still in the parking garage. He should have had ample time to make his way home since leaving the daycare.

As Cynthia pulled out of her parking spot, she saw the lights on David's Escalade flash on. Please God, pleeease let this be a coincidence. Cynthia drove to the exit, scanned her parking pass and turned right onto Fifth Avenue. She had driven a block and a half when she saw David's Escalade pull out of the parking garage a few cars behind her. He had also turned right onto Fifth Avenue. He could be going anywhere, but she knew he lived in the opposite direction. Cynthia began to panic as she realized her only way to call for help, was in her purse, locked in the trunk.

17

Oh. My. God. What do I do?! Breathe. Keep breathing.

"Mommy, I'm hungry," came from the backseat. Cynthia rummaged around in the glove box and found a granola bar and some crackers she had stashed there during her last stint working late. She passed them back to Luke, bending her arm in such a way she was still facing the road to see where she was going.

Cynthia checked the rearview mirror to find David was still a few cars behind her. She certainly didn't want him knowing where she lived—although she guessed he could find out anyway. All he would have to do is check with H.R., and they would tell him. Cynthia decided to go straight as long as she could until she figured out where to go. She was willing to drive around the block all night if that's what it took to lose David.

"Alright, sweetie, how about we put some music on?" Cynthia needed to keep up the charade that everything was fine for Luke's sake. She checked the mirror again, David was getting closer. What is he planning to do?

It was dark, and downtown was starting to get busy with business people finishing up a late meal or starting their night out with friends. The row of pubs along Fifth Avenue was lit up; their sidewalk signs invitingly set out in hopes of a busy night. Wait, is that Ben? Yes, it is! Cynthia pulled over in front of the pub as Ben was shaking hands with one fellow and simultaneously waving goodbye to someone else with the other hand. She kept her eyes on the rearview. David switched lanes to avoid the slow traffic in front of the pub but slowed down as he passed Cynthia. She avoided looking in his direction yet felt a cold and evil stare as he drove by.

Cynthia rolled down the front passenger window and called to Ben. He was already on his way over but looking in David's direction as he approached.

"Was that David Jerew?" he asked.

"Uh, I think so," Cynthia needed to keep David's threat and everything that surrounded it to herself for now, especially with Luke in the car.

"He looked really pissed. What's his problem?"

"You know how he is. He's probably just annoyed we aren't still at the office. Did you want a ride?"

"Are you sure? I can probably walk from here."

"I don't mind." Cynthia was desperate for Ben to accept her offer. Going home to find David sitting in her driveway was not something she was up for tonight. Or ever for that matter.

To Cynthia's relief, Ben got in, and she introduced him to Luke. David was long gone, but Cynthia felt much better having Ben in the car with her.

"Have you talked to the police yet?" Ben asked as Cynthia turned off Fifth.

"No," she replied and panic set in as she remembered what David said. What am I going to tell Detective Bain?

18

"I just realized I have no idea where you live," Cynthia turned to Ben as she instinctively headed out of the congested downtown core.

"I was wondering. Thought maybe you'd been stalking me," Ben joked. "I'm not too far from here. Keep going as if you're heading out of town and when you hit McKinley, I'm the next apartment building on the left. You can drop me across the street though. Turning into the parkade can be a bit of a nightmare sometimes."

Cynthia glanced in the rearview mirror and noticed Luke had fallen asleep while she and Ben were talking. Cynthia loved the lights of downtown when it was dark. Many streets and shops still had their Christmas lights up. Cynthia started to reach for the stereo just as Ben cleared his throat and looked back at Luke.

"I know I didn't really know you when Jason died, but I'm really sorry. I don't know if you know, but I worked with him a little. He was a great guy. Took the time to explain things to me. Not just how to do them but why. He was the only manager I had who did that."

"Thank you," Cynthia said, a little surprised at Ben's thoughtfulness. "He really was a great accountant. I learned a lot from working with him. We had a lot of laughs too. He had a knack for lightening up those late evenings but also taught me it didn't pay to cut corners. Ethics always come first."

To this Cynthia chuckled. "Yes, he was a stickler for ethics. Part of why he was such a well-respected accountant." Cynthia drove through the intersection at McKinley and looked for a spot to pull over. She didn't want Ben to leave. It was nice chatting with him instead of thinking about David's earlier threat. She felt safe with Ben in the car.

"You can pull over here. I'm just to the left there." Ben interrupted Cynthia's thoughts with a gesture to his left. "Thanks for the ride."

"No problem," I was going this way anyway. Actually, Cynthia wasn't going in Ben's direction but giving him a ride gave her something to do besides worry about David and what she was going to tell Detective Bain in the morning.

As she watched Ben cross the street and enter his building, she couldn't help but think about what he'd said about Jason. There was definitely no question about his ethics. He did everything by the book including how he handled their relationship. He made sure to tell H.R. as soon as he and Cynthia started dating. His ethics were so strong because his career was so important to him. What would he do if he was alive today and he was the one being threatened by David?

Cynthia was about to merge into traffic from where she had pulled over when she noticed oncoming headlights flashing at her in the rearview. Strange. I'll just wait a minute and see what that's about. As the lights got closer, Cynthia went numb when she realized the flashing lights belonged to a black Escalade. She wanted to duck down in her seat, but instead, she glanced in the back. Thankfully, Luke was still sleeping. Cynthia stared straight ahead waiting for the Escalade to pass but it never did. She thought maybe David turned off but saw him sitting in the lane next to her as she shoulder-checked to pull back onto the street. She tried to hide her fear by looking right at him. He angrily glared at her then lifted a finger to his lips as if to tell her to keep quiet. And with a screech of rubber on the pavement, he was gone.

19

Luke remained asleep while Cynthia lifted him out of his car seat and carried him into the house. She laid him on the couch because he was too heavy for her to make it all the way to his bed. She sat beside him watching him sleep noticing how peaceful he looked. She could sit there all night watching him. Cynthia was struck by how much Luke looked like Jason. She always knew he did, but tonight the resemblance was stronger than ever. Maybe it was because Cynthia was missing Jason so much or maybe it was because of the brief conversation she had with Ben about him.

What am I going to do? She thought about Jason and what he would do in her situation. She knew the truth and transparency was important to him, but she also knew how much he loved her and Luke. But Jason was an ethical person at the core. During his time as Senior Manager at D&A, Jason always stood up for what he believed in. He didn't let partners like David push him around.

Cynthia plopped down on the couch and snuggled in next to Luke. She stroked his hair and kissed him on the cheek.

"You know what you need to do, Cyn." A voice seemed to come from out of thin air. It was a voice Cynthia hadn't heard in over two years.

"Jason?"

"It's me."

"But . . . how?"

"Did you think when I died I was gone forever? I'm here in your heart and your head, and you need me now."

"I do need you. I don't know what to tell the detective tomorrow. I don't want to lose my job, and I definitely don't want anything to happen to Luke or my parents."

"I'm so sorry I never filed those life insurance papers with HR. This wouldn't be a problem for you now if I had done that years ago when we got married."

"Don't even go there. You know I'd still be working even if you had. I need to work. My career is important to me. Plus, I completely understood your fears in filing those papers. Like the minute you sent them in, something terrible would happen to you. You couldn't have known this was going to happen. None of us could. But I need to make sure Luke doesn't lose his other parent. How can I do that and still tell the truth?"

"Listen to your gut, Cyn. What is it telling you to do? You know one of the most important things about being a CPA is our fiduciary duty. Not only do we have a legal obligation to act in the best interests of our clients, but we also have a duty to the general public to be truthful in all that we do, not just our professional lives."

"Yes, I have to tell the truth. There's no question that's what I need to do, but I need to come up with a plan to protect Luke and my parents from David."

"What could David possibly do to you? He needs you to finish this audit, right?"

"You're right. He's already told me there's no option but to finish this audit on time. Ha! He's just talking out of his ass. What's he going to do, fire me during the firm's busiest audit time? There's no way he would do that! I feel so much better now. Thanks, my love, I miss you."

"Love you always, Cyn. I'm here whenever you need me."

Cynthia imagined Jason's arms wrapping around her in a big bear hug. She drifted off to sleep, confident David couldn't touch her or her family.

20

Gord flung the glass door open like it was any other day and hustled in to greet Julie. She was in Jim's office.

"Hi, Julie. How are you holding up?" Julie looked up from where she was standing behind Jim's desk. She had a pile of papers in her hands, and it looked as though she was sorting them.

"Oh, hi, Gord. As good as can be expected. You?"

"About the same. Why don't you let me clean up in here? I'll have to take over the audit contact anyway. I might as well wrap my head around where Jim was at with our financial statements."

"Thanks, Gord. The phone has been ringing off the hook. Seems like all I do is talk on the phone now."

"You were pretty close to Jim, right? How's his family taking it."

"We weren't that close, but I did meet his sister once. She's really the only family he has. I left a message for her to call me. I think she might be vacationing in L.A. Her and her husband like to go there to break up the winter. Did you know she's a CPA too?"

"No, I didn't. Funny, Jim never mentioned her to me. Thanks for all the extra time you put in yesterday. I know everything is just so . . . I don't even know how to describe it, but I appreciate you keeping things together around here."

"Thanks, boss. I'll leave you to it in here."

Gord sat down and fired up Jim's computer. He flipped through the piles of paper Julie left while he waited for the computer to boot. After noting there was nothing urgent in the pile, just a few bills to pay, he set the papers in the inbox on

Jim's desk. The computer was ready and prompting Gord for Jim's login. Shit. Where would that be? He remembered I.T. would leave the username and password under the keyboard after setting up a new employee. Jim was hardly a new employee, but Gord wasn't sure where else to look. He lifted Jim's keyboard and found a neon Post-It with a username and password scribbled on it. As bad as that would be, he only hoped Jim hadn't changed his password since this note was written. Gord quickly typed the characters then waited for confirmation from the computer. Bingo! He was in.

Had Jim still been alive, Gord would have made a note to remind him of the importance of changing his password. That was so Jim. Always said he didn't have time to come up with original passwords every month. Gord waited for the computer to give him access then started scanning Jim's documents for the audit files. As Gord scanned through the list of recently opened files, another file caught his eye. It was labeled "Environmental Matters – EG." Gord opened the document and started scanning it. It was a letter to Eve.

Dear Dr. Greenwich,

I've seen you out and about with that fancy accountant from PPC. How do you think your environmental lobbyists would feel about that? You preach about the big ugly pipeline companies ruining our land and decimating entire bird populations, and yet here you are running around with one of their key employees. I'm not sure what's worse - the fact that you're cheating on your husband or the fact that you're putting your career in jeopardy by risking getting caught with someone you claim is your enemy.

If you want your secret to remain a secret, you must stop this foolish behavior at once.

After he read the letter, Gord deleted the file but not before printing it, folding it up and putting it in his pocket. He would add it to his collection. It was time for him to ask Eve about this. He wasn't planning on covering for her forever. Maybe this was why she was acting erratically in the back alley earlier. But would she go so far as to kill Jim over this?

21

It was 10:45 a.m., Cynthia was slightly ahead of schedule to meet with Detective Bain. She sat in the reception area reading a copy of *Cosmopolitan*. It was nice to read something other than her textbooks, even if it was only for a few minutes. Cynthia felt much calmer than she had the night before. She knew there was no question she had to tell Detective Bain everything she saw.

"Ms. Webber?" Cynthia looked up from a quiz about what sleeping positions say about you and your partner. "Detective Bain will see you now."

Putting the magazine back where she got it from, Cynthia smiled and followed the receptionist to a meeting room a few doors down the hall. "Have a seat and Detective Bain will be right with you."

"Thank you."

Cynthia wished she had brought the magazine with her. She hated just sitting and waiting. There was an unopened bottle of water on her side of the table. She assumed it was for her, opened it, and took a good long drink. As she set the bottle down, Detective Bain entered the room and sat down across from her.

"Randy Bain," the detective said as he held out his hand for Cynthia to shake it. Cynthia extended her hand in return and said, "Cynthia Webber, nice to meet you." Randy and Cynthia sat down and got straight to business discussing the discovery of Jim's body. Detective Bain informed Cynthia that this was a formal statement and even though some of the questions had already been answered by other witnesses, he still had to ask them.

"I understand you were at Prairie Pipeline Company when their CFO, Gordon James, discovered the body of Jim Dunn, PPC's controller?"

"Yes, I was at PPC when Jim's body was discovered but . . ."

"And what were you doing at PPC that morning?"

"I was conducting an inventory count for their financial statement audit."

"And where were you when Mr. James discovered the body?"

"Actually, Mr. James didn't discover the body. I did."

"You discovered Jim Dunn's body?"

"Yes."

"Could you elaborate because I have a whole testimony from Mr. James stating that he was the one who discovered Mr. Dunn's body?"

"I'm not sure why Gord . . . ah, Mr. James, said he discovered Jim's body. Even that day I was confused by why he said that, but it was like my mouth wouldn't move to speak up and say that I was the one who found the body." Cynthia remembered all the emotions she felt when she discovered Jim's body just a couple of days ago.

"I felt like maybe Mr. James was trying to be nice after seeing the state I was in. But I couldn't let the investigation continue with information I knew was false. I found the body after discovering a shoe in the yard which I later learned was Jim's. He was in one of the pipes."

"And where did you find Mr. Dunn's body?"

"As I mentioned, I was counting the pipes that day. He was tucked in there so neatly as if he was put there to sleep for the night, but once I climbed in the pipe to see if he was okay, it was clear he wasn't, and he never would be."

Cynthia tried to compose herself. but the thought of seeing Jim the way she had was too much. She grabbed a tissue from the box on the table and wiped her eyes while she tried to steady her breathing. Detective Bain let her have a minute and then pressed on. "Are you okay to continue, Ms. Webber?"

"Yes, I'm fine. I just never imagined I'd be finding dead bodies in my line of work. Accounting is normally pretty uneventful, you know."

"Oh, you'd be surprised," Detective Bain muttered almost inaudibly. Cynthia wondered what he meant by that and assumed it had something to do with financial crimes rather than homicides. "Was there anything else in the pipe with Mr. Dunn?"

"Yes. I saw something sparkle on Mr. Dunn's collar. I think it was an earring, but I couldn't get close enough to tell for sure."

"Right. I remember reading that in the crime scene report." Detective Bain made some notes on the yellow legal pad on the table in front of him. "Did you notice anything else that might help us?"

"I don't think so. Once I realized he wasn't breathing, I was pretty quick to get out of the pipe and run to the office. My cell phone was in the office. I figured either someone would see me yelling and running and call 9-1-1 or I would call 9-1-1 once I made it inside."

"And it was Ms. Mann who called 9-1-1, is that correct?"

"Yes."

"How would you describe your relationship with the deceased?"

"I didn't really know him. I met him a couple of months ago at PPC when my audit team and I went there for a meeting at the start of the interim audit. I got the impression he spent all his time at the office. Julie . . . ah, Ms. Mann would know more about him. She's the assistant controller and spent a lot of time at the office with him, I think."

"Do you think Ms. Mann would have any reason to want Jim dead? Will she be moving into the position of Controller now that Jim's gone?"

"I never really thought about that. I guess she probably would. Or maybe PPC would advertise the position. I guess that would be up to the board of directors."

"And what about Mr. James, is there any reason you know of that he would want Mr. Dunn out of the picture?"

"No, Jim was pretty integral to the company. I'd imagine now that he's gone, it's created a lot more work for Mr. James."

"Thank you, Ms. Webber. I have no further questions for you today, but I'll be in touch if anything else comes up. Thank you for coming in."

As Cynthia left the precinct, she had a strange feeling someone was watching her. She realized how ridiculous this was but still walked faster and faster until she got to her car. She quickly jumped in and closed the door. Only after she'd locked the doors did she take a deep breath and look around to see if someone was following her. She remembered David's threat and laughed to herself thinking there was no way he would hurt her family.

22

Gord was anxiously awaiting a response to the text he'd sent Eve after discovering the blackmail letter on Jim's computer. It wasn't the first one he'd found. Several months ago, he found a similar letter in Jim's office when he was working late alone in the office. He needed some reports from Jim's office and accidentally discovered the letter next to Jim's "secret" bottle of Crown Royal in his desk drawer. That letter was different. It reminded him of something a kidnapper might send with letters cut out of a magazine and glued in place. Gord wondered if, over time, Jim's letters had become more threatening because Eve clearly didn't care to discuss them with him. Maybe she was scared. Or maybe she had talked to the police, but they couldn't do anything. Either way, Gord didn't realize Jim was still threatening Eve. He couldn't shake the suspicion she was somehow involved in Jim's death.

Gord's phone blipped, and he glanced at it to see it was Eve.

I told you we're done, the text read. Gord composed a reply telling Eve he knew about the blackmail.

Are you nuts? Not over the phone! Eve responded. *Meet me at our old spot in an hour.*

Ok. Gord put his phone in his pocket. He checked the time on his computer. It was 11:40 a.m. He had time to grab lunch before meeting Eve. He left his office and walked down the hall towards the main reception area and Julie's desk.

"I'm taking an early lunch and then I have a meeting downtown. I'll be back in a couple of hours."

"See you later," Julie said as she picked up the phone to call one of PPC's satellite offices in Red Deer.

Gord arrived at the secret meeting spot with time to spare. Copperfield Park was about as far away from downtown as you could get in the city. It was also quite close to where construction on PPC's new pipeline had started across Highway 22. It was ironic this had become Gord and Eve's usual meeting spot considering Eve and her supporters were so dead set against this project. Gord headed to the back of the park and found the big oak tree where he and Eve first met.

As Gord finished his takeout, he saw Eve marching towards him. She did not look impressed. Gord stood up, hoping that would put him on equal footing with Eve, but it was clear she wasn't going to calm down anytime soon.

"What the hell, Gord?"

"What do you mean what the hell? I'm the one who should be asking you that! The man who was blackmailing you turns up dead, and you're not a bit worried?"

"I'm not worried because I didn't have anything to do with Jim's death."

"Why didn't you tell me he was blackmailing you? I could have talked to that drunk and made him stop."

"Right, and confirm he was right about us. That's the last thing I wanted to do. How did he find out about us anyway? I've never even been to your office. That's the last place I'd want to be seen with all the trouble your company's causing in this city."

"Trouble? Really? You think providing thousands of jobs is trouble? Not to mention the good we've done for the country with all the other pipelines we've built. We're a responsible company, Eve. We make sure to displace as little wildlife as possible, and our reclamation process is second to none."

"So, what are you planning to do with those letters? Where are they now?" Eve was starting to look frantic. "They're not yours, and they have nothing to do with you."

"Wait, nothing to do with me? We have sex for months, and these letters have nothing to do with me? I cover for you in a murder investigation, and these letters have nothing to do with me." Gord was hissing like a snake at this point. He wanted to yell at the top of his lungs he was so infuriated but he didn't want to attract the attention of anyone who might be in the park. "You know what, Eve? I'm going to keep those letters. I think they might come in handy."

"Real mature, Gord. You know I had nothing to do with Jim's murder."

"I don't actually. You had a lot to gain by getting him out of the picture. It would have been your reputation in the gutter had this city found out you were sleeping with the enemy. Not that I see it that way. I love you, Eve."

"If you really love me then give me those letters."

"I don't have them here. Don't worry, they're safe, and I'll keep them safe until I have a reason not to."

"Is that a threat?"

Gord didn't answer.

23

Cynthia stopped for lunch on her way back to the office. She was happy with how her meeting with Detective Bain had gone. She knew David would be pissed but felt like he was powerless over her during this busy audit season. She was already doing more work than she was responsible for because D&A was so short-staffed. She pulled into her spot in the parkade and headed upstairs to resume her work on the PPC audit. She thought about stopping by Little Seedlings to say hi to Luke but felt like the stop at the police station had already taken enough time out of her work day. She would rather get back to work and be able to pick Luke up earlier.

The elevator dinged, and Cynthia stepped out to see David chatting with Sheryl. Part of her wanted to step back into the elevator and disappear until David had cleared the reception area but it was too late, David had already made eye contact with her. Cynthia opted to go the long way to her desk, so she wouldn't have to walk by David and Sheryl. Ben caught up with Cynthia on her way to her desk to find out what she wanted him to work on that day. He spent the morning working on checklists and thought the audit was in pretty good shape.

Cynthia and Ben arrived at Cynthia's workstation as Cynthia finished giving him his instructions for the next step in completing the audit. They would have yet another meeting with Sam and the rest of the audit team later that day. Ben headed off to his desk while Cynthia unpacked her laptop and got ready to get back to work. She was about to sit down when she heard David's voice from behind her.

"Ms. Webber." Cynthia felt like a child whose mother was using their full name because they were in big trouble.

"Hi, David. How are you this afternoon?" Cynthia tried to lighten the mood.

"I know what you did," David said, ignoring Cynthia's question. "I know you talked to that detective this morning and I've arranged for security to escort you out of the building."

"But . . ."

"No buts, Ms. Webber. I warned you what would happen if you talked to the police." David made sure to keep his voice down. Cynthia saw a security officer arriving in the hallway behind David. It was Jeff. He was a regular in the building, and Cynthia had chatted with him a number of times when she'd had to work late. David turned to Jeff. "Escort this woman out of the building. She no longer works here."

"Yes, sir," Jeff replied. Cynthia was stunned and frozen in place, yet she was thankful David had stormed off, leaving Jeff to deal with her.

"It's okay, Cynthia, take your time collecting your things. I know this is unexpected." All kinds of thoughts were rushing through Cynthia's mind. Most of all, she didn't understand why David was doing this. She didn't understand why, as a CPA, a professional who has a fiduciary duty to the public, David would interfere with her telling the truth about what happened at PPC. She'd guessed it had to do with PPC being David's largest client, but there was no covering up the fact that a body was discovered onsite. Cynthia didn't see what difference it made to David that she saw an earring on Jim's body.

Cynthia took a deep gasping breath as she remembered David's threat to her family. Panic struck her as she worried for Luke's safety. Jeff must have heard her gasp for air.

"Are you alright, Ms. Webber?"

"Yes, I just need to get down to the daycare as soon as

possible. I need to see my son."

"I understand."

There wasn't much for Cynthia to pack from her desk. Because she spent a lot of time at clients' offices, Cynthia's belongings all fit in her laptop backpack which was supplied by D&A. Her laptop. She realized this was no longer hers but that it was the property of D&A. She removed her wallet from the backpack and left the backpack on her desk. She wanted to talk to Ben, Ryan, and Sam and explain to them what was going on, but she knew even though Jeff was a kind and understanding man, he wouldn't allow this.

"Alright, I think I've got everything," Cynthia said to Jeff as the pair headed to the elevator.

The elevator arrived at the 21st floor, and Cynthia felt queasy as she let her emotions get out of hand worrying about Luke's safety.

"Luke!" she called, but she didn't see him anywhere.

"Hi, Cynthia," Rachel said walking towards Cynthia. "Luke's not here. I just got back from my lunch break. I had assumed you picked Luke up while I was at lunch." Rachel stopped talking as she noticed Jeff behind Cynthia. "What's going on?" Rachel asked slowly as if she didn't really want to know the answer. She knew what it meant to be escorted out of the building by security.

"I've been fired. I need to see Luke. Where is he? WHO HAS HIM?!" Cynthia screamed as her panic level heightened.

"Hold on. I wasn't here when he was picked up. Let me check." Rachel disappeared to find out who picked Luke up. Cynthia felt hot tears on her cheeks as she imagined the worst. She was sure David had made good on his threat and taken Luke. She saw Rachel walking back towards her. "Um, I don't know how this happened."

"Oh my god, you let David take him, didn't you?" Cynthia shrieked at Rachel.

"Actually, we don't know who took Luke. Many of us were on our lunch break, and we have a new care provider. She forgot to sign Luke out, so we don't know who picked him up or at what time."

"Surely she can describe the person who picked him up."

"She's gone for lunch. I'm so sorry, Cynthia. This should never have happened."

"What about someone else? Did anyone else see who picked Luke up?" Cynthia cried. She covered her mouth as she tried to calm herself down and breathe.

"Nobody else saw Luke leave. They were busy with the other children."

"How is that possible? I don't understand," Cynthia cried. She wanted to grab her cell phone to call her parents, but she realized it was in the laptop backpack on her desk.

"As soon as Carrie's back from lunch I'll call you."

"You'll have to call my home. Can I borrow your phone? Maybe my mom has Luke."

"Of course." Rachel handed Cynthia the portable phone. Cynthia dialed her parents' phone number, but there was no answer.

"I've got to go. I need to find Luke." Cynthia said through tears.

"I'm so sorry. Don't worry, Cynthia. Nobody would have let him leave with anyone other than someone on your list."

Cynthia took a deep breath. She tried to feel comforted by this fact, but she didn't understand how it was possible that nobody saw Luke leave. Another worker came from the back carrying Luke's backpack. She gave it to Cynthia as Cynthia tried to calm down.

"Ms. Webber." Cynthia jumped as Jeff put his hand on her shoulder. "Why don't we head to your car then you can get home and figure out where your boy is."

"Yes, of course. I need to get home." Cynthia turned to Rachel, "I've got to go. Please call me at home if anybody remembers anything."

"Of course, Cynthia. I'm so sorry!"

Jeff escorted Cynthia down to the parkade and took her

parking pass and key card. As Cynthia handed Jeff her key card, she completely lost it and broke down sobbing all the while apologizing to Jeff for being so emotional.

"It's okay, Ms. Webber. I'll miss seeing you around."

"It won't be for long if I have anything to say about it." Cynthia was suddenly extremely calm, and a look of sheer determination came over her face. "First, I'm going to find my son, and then I'm getting to the bottom of this. I've done nothing wrong. I understand you're just doing your job," Cynthia said as she stormed off towards her car. Soon Jeff was standing alone watching Cynthia's tail lights disappear out of the parkade and onto the street.

Cynthia gasped as she rounded the block and neared her driveway. Oh my god! she thought. It can't be! Her car had barely rolled into park when Cynthia jumped out, leaving the driver's door open. "Luke?!" she screamed at the top of her lungs. She burst through the door, and Gayle looked up from the couch where she and Luke sat reading a book.

"What's the matter, dear. What are you doing home so early?" Gayle could tell Cynthia was clearly distraught.

"Luke, I thought you were gone," Cynthia said without thinking.

"Gone where, Mommy?"

"I went to pick you up, and you weren't there, so I thought you were lost."

"Grandma picked me up," Luke said looking at Gayle. Cynthia looked at Gayle with an annoyed look in her eyes.

"Don't you remember asking me to get Luke yesterday? You thought you might be working late and it would be good for Luke to be home at the regular time. I decided to take him out for lunch and then it just didn't make sense to take him back to the daycare. I hope you don't mind, dear."

"Of course, not. It must have slipped my mind."

"Well, you have had a lot going on the last couple of days. Are you okay? You didn't answer me before. Why are you home so early?"

"You won't believe it. I can hardly believe it myself. David fired me."

"What?! After what happened to you? How can he do that?"

"He can't, Mom. I intend to fight it. But I need to figure out why. I just don't understand. He was mad I talked to the police. Or, I should say he was mad I told the truth about what I saw. They're his top client, but it just doesn't make sense. Why wouldn't he want me to tell the truth?"

"Well, honey, you know there can be a bad bunch in any profession."

"Yeah, I guess," Cynthia shrugged and shook her head, but she was still so confused by the last couple of days' activities. She didn't want to think about it right now. What mattered most was that Luke was safe. At least David hadn't followed through on the threat to her family. Not yet, anyway. Cynthia turned to Gayle, "I'm glad you and Luke got to have a lunch date. He misses you."

24

Eve rushed back to the university, still fuming from her meeting with Gord. She had borrowed April's car again just to be safe, and once again she made up some lame excuse why she couldn't take the train. She told April she was going to check out the site where PPC was starting to set up construction for the pipeline south of the city. While it was just a line at the time, Eve did end up driving by the construction site.

"Did you hear anything about what's going on at PPC's construction site? I drove by there and saw some emergency crews. Was there a protest going on there this afternoon?"

"Not that I know of. Kurt didn't mention anything to me." Eve knew April liked to go to as many protests as possible. Eve did too, but she felt like she had to keep it a little lower key given her position of seniority at the university.

"Let me know as soon as you hear something, okay?"

"Of course." April was always happy to help Eve out.

"By the way, do you have some heels I can borrow for the staff dinner Friday? Your shoes are so much cuter than mine. It's a shame you can't make it."

April glanced at the heels under her desk. "I'll make it to the next one. I do love a free dinner. I'll bring you some shoes tomorrow." April hesitated. "I'm working on your statement for the Friday news. I'm planning to highlight the murder at PPC and how that's just one more reason for the pipeline construction to be shut down."

"No. No, don't do that," Eve said, thinking about Gord and his threats. "I want you to focus on the damage the pipeline will do to the environment and the habitats in the south. PPC will get enough bad press around the murder. I'm sure the media will handle that aspect for us."

"Okay, whatever you say." April was a bit surprised given that Eve usually liked to include as much information as possible in her statements to make PPC look bad. April went to her computer and found the local news to see if there was anything she could learn about PPC's construction site. She also tried Kurt's cell but there was no answer, and his voicemail was full.

* * *

"Hello," Cynthia said as she picked up her phone.

"Hi, Cynthia. It's Rachel from Little Seedlings. I wanted to let you know Carrie said it was your mom who picked up Luke."

"Yes, she was here with him when I got home. Thank you."

"I'm sorry it took me so long to get back to you. I know that was hours ago, but we've just been so swamped and short-staffed here."

"That's alright. Well, I guess I won't be seeing you until I get this mess sorted out with D&A. Thank you for taking such good care of Luke. I really appreciate it."

"We'll really miss him. He's such a good kid."

"Thanks. I'll let him know you said that. Bye." The back door flung open as Cynthia was hanging up the phone. It was Linda, and she had that crazed look in her eye when she was working on a hot story. Because Linda and Cynthia were best friends and told each other everything, knowing the other wouldn't say anything, Cynthia often got details about things she probably shouldn't. She didn't mind. It was a good release for Linda.

"Sit the fu . . . oh, hi, Luke. Hi, Mrs. Roberts." Linda stopped herself before she said something inappropriate. "Cyn, you are not going to believe what just happened. They found another body on PPC property. Out at the construction site along the 22X Highway." Linda lowered her voice as she and Cynthia continued to Cynthia's room.

"Are you messing with me?" Cynthia remembered the games Linda used to play with her when they were roommates in university. Linda was such a good storyteller Cynthia believed everything she told her, but after a while, she figured out Linda would make stuff up just to see if it was believable. She liked testing her stories out on Cynthia.

"No, way! Have I ever joked about murder before?"

"Well, no, but there hasn't really been an occasion to joke about it before. Not that it's a joking matter now, either. What's going on?"

"Police think it's a well-known activist. Kurt Ripple. Looks like PPC's going to be out of business for a while. That construction site will be out of commission until they figure out what happened. Gunshot wound this time."

"What?" Cynthia sat with her mouth gaping. She couldn't believe it.

"Well, so much for David and his attempts to protect PPC."

"What do you mean?"

"He threatened me not to tell the police the truth about what I saw on Monday. He didn't want them to know about the earring, I guess. It's so weird. I saw Detective Bain this morning and told him the truth. When I got back to the office, David had me escorted out of the building. I'm officially unemployed."

"Are you shitting me?! That's ridiculous. What is David's problem? Why would he care?"

"That's what I don't understand. Can you help me find out? I know you don't like to use your sources for personal gain but . . ."

"Stop. You know I have strict rules about my sources but what David's done to you is pretty newsworthy. If I knew how this was connected to Jim's murder, it would be one of my top stories. A long time exemplary employee getting fired just for telling the truth that doesn't in any way implicate her company or her boss. That sure raises some suspicions as to David's involvement in this whole thing. You bet your ass I'm going to find out what his stake in all this is, Cyn."

"Thank you. If you need any help with research, I've got a lot of extra time on my hands now. All I have to do is study for the CPA exam. It's not like getting fired from one of the city's top accounting firms is going to land me a lot of job offers."

"We'll get to the bottom of this. You were fired without just cause, and there are penalties and repercussions for that. I've got to get ready to go live and report about this second body, but I'm seeing Troy later tonight. I'm sure he'll have some information for me about Jim's cause of death. I'll call you later."

"Just call me in the morning and enjoy your date with Troy." Cynthia knew how busy Linda was and she didn't get a lot of time for dating. Troy worked at the Medical Examiner's office, and he was keen to help Linda out when he could.

"Alright, thanks, Cyn."

"You might want to call my parents instead of the house. I'm not sure how much time I will be spending here considering David's threats. I would feel a little better if Luke and I were somewhere David couldn't find us too easily. To top everything off, I left my cell phone at D&A."

"Okay, I'll talk to you tomorrow, and we'll figure out a game plan," Linda said authoritatively as she headed out towards the back door. She gave Luke and Gayle each a hug and was on her way.

25

David sat in his office watching many of the staff from the audit department walk by in the hallway as they got ready to leave for the day. He got up from his desk and walked over to his door. He didn't care for the open-door policy many of the other partners seemed to like so much. David closed his door and looked around his barren office. He was married and divorced three times and had two children but you couldn't tell from looking around his office. There were no photos or other evidence of his family anywhere.

David was the kind of partner that articling students dreaded. He had no qualms about writing "wtf" on working papers and calculations that weren't up to his standards. He was thankful he no longer had much contact with students. He preferred to wine and dine his clients and figure out who to prospect next. David ate out about 90% of the time and when he did eat at home it was something he could simply heat up.

He contemplated the day's events. He'd met with Sam and the PPC audit team that afternoon and informed them that Cynthia no longer worked at D&A. That's all he said. He didn't give any details and didn't answer any of the questions the team had. Most of them wanted to know if Cynthia was okay and why she no longer worked at D&A. David deflected their questions, telling the team they'd have to ask Cynthia. They knew Cynthia though and knew she would never quit during busy season even after discovering a dead body on the job.

The team was given strict orders to finish the audit as soon as possible. Tonight even. David implied they should take any shortcuts necessary. Sam protested. He would rather stay up all night than risk taking shortcuts that could have serious consequences for his career.

As David looked out the window and observed the setting sun against the snowy backdrop of winter, he smiled inside knowing he was in complete control. He pulled out his cell phone and checked for messages. There was a text that caught his attention. It simply said, *It's done*. David smiled to himself as he read it. Soon this mess with PPC would be behind him.

* * *

April also sat in her office with the door closed. She was watching the news, unable to take her eyes off Linda Reeves at the PPC construction site. She thought she heard wrong. She thought Linda said the man she'd been dating for the last three months was found at the construction site with a gunshot wound in the back of his head. April couldn't believe it. There had to be some sort of mistake. Kurt had always stood up for what he believed in. He didn't deserve to die like this, and for what? All because he wasn't afraid to express his opinion, to try and stop the harm that would come to the city if the pipeline was successfully constructed.

Tears flowed steadily down April's cheeks. She was unable to move and get a Kleenex, so she wiped her nose with her sleeve. She knew Eve would want to know what happened, but she wanted to get herself under control first. Nobody really knew about her and Kurt, and she wasn't ready to tell anyone just yet. She didn't like to share her opinions as freely as Kurt did and it was for that reason she hadn't told any of her friends they were dating.

A knock on the door startled April.

"April, I'm heading home now," Eve said from the other side of the door. "I'll see you tomorrow." April took a deep breath realizing she wouldn't see Kurt tomorrow. She wouldn't see him ever again.

"See you tomorrow," she said.

"Let me know what you find out about that construction site," Eve said as she left. April closed her eyes and wondered why Kurt would be at the construction site by himself. She wondered how Eve would react to the news of an activist and fellow university professor being gunned down at the site of the pipeline. Eve would get revenge. No matter how April looked at it, she knew Eve would find a way to make sure PPC paid for what happened to Kurt. It was more fuel for the fire that would destroy PPC. Somehow this thought calmed April. She knew she had to find out what happened to Kurt so she could pass the information on to Eve and strengthen her case against the pipeline. She owed it to Kurt for keeping her secret. She started working on a new speech. She knew Eve would want to address this tomorrow when she heard the news of Kurt's death.

26

"**I'd like to provide** an anonymous tip, please," Gord spoke into his cell phone. He was jittery from skipping dinner. News of the second body connected to PPC had him furious. He felt like this had gone beyond the problems the protesters had with the pipeline. It felt personal to him. He had invested everything into his career at PPC, and he wasn't about to stand by and let this company go to hell.

"One moment, please," the operator on the other end of the line replied. "Alright, go ahead, sir."

"Yes, I have some information that may be connected to the murders at PPC. I believe Dr. Eve Greenwich may have something to do with them."

"Eve Greenwich? The environmental scientist?"

"Yes, I have evidence proving she was being blackmailed by the first murder victim."

"May I have your name, sir."

"No, I said I wanted to this tip to be anonymous. You'll receive a package at the station within the hour. The package will contain all the evidence I have. If you don't receive the package before noon, I want you to call this number." Gord had purchased a burner phone for the sole purpose of calling in his tip. There was no way he wanted anything coming back to him. He had worked way too hard to get caught up in murder allegations.

"Okay, thank you, sir." The operator hesitated a bit, not sure if this was a joke. "Was that all, sir?"

"Yes, thank you. I just wanted to give you a heads up that you'd be receiving a package." Gord clicked his phone off before the operator could ask any more questions. He put on a pair of plastic gloves and took out all the blackmail letters he'd saved. He knew his fingerprints were already on the letters, but he hoped there would be more prints from Jim and Eve. He had no way of knowing if these letters had been sent to Eve and given back to Jim or if they were copies Jim had made. Gord could see Eve figuring out it was Jim who was blackmailing her and throwing them in his face as if to let him know she wasn't the least bit threatened. Not much got past her. Gord remembered thinking Eve didn't seem the least bit surprised when he said he found the letters in Jim's office. It's why he began to suspect Eve's involvement in the murders.

Now that there was a second body, Gord was scared Eve had killed one of her own to make it look like revenge for Jim's murder. He couldn't go to the police and risk being linked to the case through his involvement with Eve. Gord lived a few blocks from the YMCA. He concealed his envelope of letters inside his coat and walked straight there. There were always teenagers hanging around out front, and he knew one of them would be eager to make a few bucks. He offered $50 to the first teen he saw with a bike that made eye contact with him.

"Take this to the police station and give it to the receptionist. Ask her to write, 'I received your package' on this piece of paper. If she doesn't receive the package before noon, she'll be calling me on this phone. Meet me back here when you're done."

"No problem, man. The police station's only about ten blocks away. I'll see you in fifteen minutes." Gord thought fifteen minutes was a little overzealous, but he gave the teen the benefit of the doubt. He went into the Y to get a cup of coffee and read the paper while he waited. He sat down next to a window where he could see the meeting place in case the teen actually made it back in fifteen minutes.

27

Back at Cynthia's parents' house, Gayle and Bob were settling in for the night. Luke had fallen asleep on the drive over. Cynthia had carried him as far as the couch, and there he lied sleeping as peaceful as ever. Cynthia was glad the events of the past few days weren't affecting Luke the way they were affecting her. She felt like she was living in a bad dream and would wake up at any minute. She remembered feeling much the same way when Jason died. Everything seemed surreal. Here she was, an unemployed single mom.

"Cynthia," Gayle whispered as she poked her head out of her bedroom. Cynthia looked up at her mom. "I forgot to tell you your co-worker, Ben, called. There was a message on the voicemail. He must have kept our number after you ended up in the hospital. He sounded worried about you, dear. I wanted to make sure you got the message."

"Thanks, Mom. I'll give him a call. He's probably just wondering why I wasn't at work this afternoon. They were having a big audit team meeting."

"Don't worry, honey. This is all going to work out like it's supposed to."

"I know, Mom." Cynthia knew as traumatic and confusing this week had been so far, it was nothing compared to losing the love of her life. If she could survive that, she felt she could survive anything.

Cynthia realized in all the time she'd worked with Ben she didn't have his number. Well, she did, but it was programmed into her cell phone, so she'd never needed to memorize it. Now that she didn't have a cell, she felt a bit out of touch with all the contacts she had in it. She picked up Gayle and Bob's phone and scrolled through the call display looking for Ben's number. When she found it, she pressed auto dial, and the phone started ringing.

"Hey, Cynthia!" Cynthia wondered how Ben knew it was her. He must have recognized her parents' phone number.

"Hi, Ben. How are you?"

"I'm fine, but what's going on? David was so elusive at our meeting this afternoon. As usual, he acted like he didn't have to tell the rest of us anything, so we were wondering what happened to you. We all know you wouldn't desert us when we're so close to being done this audit. Are you okay?"

"I'll be fine. I'm a bit shocked right now, but I'll get over it. David fired me. Had me escorted out of the building and everything."

"Holy shit! He can't do that. You're one of D&A's star employees. He's got to be losing it."

"Oh, he's definitely losing it, but you didn't hear that from me. There's a lot you don't know. Just be careful around David. Keep your head down and get the job done." Cynthia wanted to tell Ben about the second body found at the PPC construction site, but she wasn't sure if Linda had gone live with the news yet, so she kept her mouth shut.

"Well, I'm going to miss working with you. I appreciate that you covered for Ryan and me. I feel like it's our fault you got fired. If there's anything I can do to make it up to you, just say the word."

"Oh, geez, it's definitely not your fault. Sure, maybe one of you might have discovered Jim's body instead, but you're not the ones making David act like a power-hungry control freak. You have nothing to do with how he acts. I'm serious though, be careful around him. He's a loose cannon right now."

"Clearly!"

"Thanks, Ben. I'm going to try and get some studying done before bed. I guess I'll see you around . . . or maybe not. Sorry, I'm not sure how all this looks for me just yet."

"I'm sure we'll see each other. If not before the exam, I'll definitely see you then."

"True enough. At least I have lots of time to study now."

"If you ever want to study with Ryan and me, you know where to find us."

"Thanks, Ben. I'll talk to you later."

"Okay, take care, Cynthia." Cynthia glanced over at Luke as she hung up the phone. He was still sleeping soundly on the couch covered in one of Gayle's knitted afghans. Cynthia decided to leave him there rather than risk taking him to bed and waking him up. The room she was staying in was just off the living room anyway. She decided to take a bath before bed to try and calm her nerves.

The guest room Cynthia and Luke were sharing had an en-suite with a soaker tub. Cynthia saw that Gayle had just stocked up on Epsom salts and there were a few candles placed around the edge of the tub. Cynthia turned on the water and went to the kitchen to see if she could find any white wine. She took the last of some Pinot Grigio that was in the door of the fridge, poured it into a fancy glass, and wandered back to the bath. Cynthia lit the candles, took off her clothes, and gracefully climbed into the tub with the water still running. She left both the bedroom and bathroom doors open so she could hear Luke if he stirred. She knew both her parents were asleep and they would never walk in on her unless it were an emergency.

Cynthia turned off the tap and took a sip of wine before letting her head rest back against the tub. The water was nice and hot. She imagined she was on a tropical island somewhere relaxing with Jason. The beach was white, and the water was turquoise. It was a place she liked to escape to whenever she could. She felt safe there, and for now, she felt safe at Gayle and Bob's.

28

April was finishing up Eve's speech. She wanted to work on it while her emotions were high after learning about Kurt's death. She knew the speech would be much more raw and effective that way. Eve would probably call a press conference as quickly as possible. April tried to keep the tears from coming as she finished proofreading the speech out loud for any spelling or grammar mistakes. As she looked up from her desk to grab another Kleenex, she noticed a vehicle in the parking lot. It was getting late, and there weren't too many vehicles left outside. She had seen this SUV before though. It was a black Escalade. She wasn't sure, but she thought someone was sitting inside. Her eyes were still blurry from the tears, and it was far enough away that it was hard to focus on the interior. She assumed it was another university employee working late.

"Miss Sundin?" April nearly jumped out of her skin when she heard a knock on her office door which was normally left open. She recognized the voice as belonging to Gerry, one of the campus security officers. She opened the door as she wiped her eyes one more time with her Kleenex.

"Hi, Gerry."

"Miss Sundin, are you alright? You don't look well."

"I was just watching the news about Kurt, one of the professors here. He was killed tonight and was a good friend of mine."

"I'm so sorry to hear that, Miss Sundin. Did you need a ride home?"

"I'll be fine, thank you, Gerry."

"Alright, well, when you do decide to head home for the night, please call campus security to walk you to your car. I don't mean to scare you, but there's been a suspicious vehicle spotted on campus. We are checking into it, but we are also warning anyone who is still working to call us for an escort no matter how far they may need to go."

"Thanks, Gerry. I usually call campus security anyway. You can never be too careful."

"Smart thinking, miss. Any one of us will be happy to escort you when you're ready."

"Okay, I'll see you soon, I'm just about finished for the night."

"I'll tell you what, I have a few more people to see in this building, and then I'll come back and see if you're ready to go."

"Thanks, Gerry," April said as she watched Gerry carry on down the hall. She wondered if the suspicious vehicle he mentioned was the black Escalade and tried to remember where she had seen it before.

29

Cynthia was up bright and early studying at the kitchen table while Gayle hustled around the kitchen getting coffee started. Bob and Gayle were always up early. Luke had already had his breakfast, and he and Bob were playing in the living room with some wooden trains Bob and Gayle kept at their place for the times Luke visited. There was a knock on the door that made Cynthia feel a little uneasy.

"I think it's for you, dear," Gayle said happily.

"What makes you think that?" Cynthia said as she got up from the table.

"Oh, a mother knows."

"Whatever that means," Cynthia said as she looked through the peephole, expecting to see Linda. It was Ben. She opened the door as Ben handed her a box of muffins.

"I hope you don't mind me stopping by. Your mom said blueberry is your favourite."

"Oh, she did, did she?" Cynthia blushed as she said it, wondering when she and Ben had the opportunity to discuss her taste in muffins.

"Yes, I called to make sure it was okay that I stopped by. I wanted to see for myself that you were doing alright."

"Cynthia, don't be rude," Gayle interrupted. Cynthia hadn't realized they were standing in the doorway talking while a brisk winter wind had picked up outside.

"Right. Come in, Ben. Sit down. My mom just put some coffee on. Have you two met? This is my mom, Gayle."

"We've just spoken on the phone," Ben answered. Before sitting down with Cynthia, he walked over to Gayle, shook her hand, and told her it was a pleasure to meet her. As Ben was introducing himself to Gayle, Bob and Luke walked over from the living room.

"Hi, Ben. I'm Bob, and this is Luke."

"Nice to meet you, Bob. Luke and I have actually met before. How's it going, bud?" Ben said holding out his hand for Luke to fist bump it.

"Alright. Well, Luke and I are going to get back to our trains."

"But I want a muffin," Luke protested.

"I did bring a chocolate chip one just for you," Ben said. That made both Luke and Cynthia smile. Cynthia opened the box of muffins and noticed Ben had brought enough for everyone and then some.

"Are you expecting more people?" Cynthia asked but then thought she might have sounded rude. "I'm sorry, I didn't mean to be rude. There's just a lot of muffins here."

"In my family, we always make sure to have plenty of food when there's a crisis. It's just the way I deal with . . . situations." Ben wasn't sure how to refer to Cynthia being fired without upsetting her. "I thought something serious must have happened for you to be fired. You're one of D&A's top employees. The other night when you and Luke gave me a ride home, I got the feeling something was wrong, but I wasn't sure if it was my place to ask."

"You know, there was something wrong. Why don't I tell you about it later? I'm sure you have to get to work." Cynthia gave Ben a look that let him know she didn't want to talk about it in front of Luke. She wasn't sure if Ben had understood, but judging from the look on his face, he had. Cynthia didn't want to keep secrets from Luke, but she also didn't want him knowing about things that weren't appropriate for kids.

"You're right. I should probably get going. Do you want to meet me for an early lunch? How about Scarpino's Deli on 10th?"

"Oh, uh." Cynthia was a bit surprised Ben wanted to talk so soon.

"Come on. It'll be my treat." Ben wanted to add, "Since you're unemployed now," but he felt it was probably too soon for that and he really didn't know Cynthia that well.

"Okay, it's a date." Cynthia felt her face flush instantly. "I mean, it's not a date. Um." Cynthia felt herself getting redder.

"It's a date," Ben winked at Cynthia as he said it. Cynthia laughed to cover up her embarrassment, but she found herself wondering if Ben really thought of it as a date or if he was just being nice. Cynthia never considered dating after Jason died. Her sole focus was always Luke.

"Wow, busy place today," Gayle said looking out the window. "Looks like Linda's just in time for coffee and a muffin."

"I should get to the office," Ben said getting up from the table as Linda came bursting through the door.

"Good morning. Oh, hello," Linda said looking at Ben. "Linda Reeves," she said extending her hand to Ben.

"Ben Wilson. Nice to meet you. Hey, you're on the news, aren't you?"

"That's me," Linda beamed. She loved it when people recognized her.

"It was nice meeting all of you. I better be on my way. Cynthia, I'll see you later. Good-bye, Luke. Take good care of your mom," Ben said as he walked out the door, still open from Linda's arrival. Linda turned to Cynthia with a quizzical look on her face.

"Who was *that*? Oh, wait, he's not the party animal, Ben, from your audit team is he?"

"Yes, that's him," Cynthia rolled her eyes at Linda. She felt a little bad for calling Ben a party animal.

"And what is he going to see you later about?"

"We're meeting for lunch. He wants to know what's going on with . . ."

"It's a date," Gayle interjected.

"It's not a date, Mom. Ben just said that because he could see it was awkward for me."

"Why are you blushing then?" Linda said adding fuel to the fire.

"You two are terrible. He's just a guy I work with."

"You seem to have a history with men you work with," Linda said taking it too far. "I'm sorry, that was uncalled for."

"It's okay, I know you didn't mean anything by it," Cynthia said like it was no big deal. "What are you doing here, anyway?"

"Remember, I was out with Troy last night. I have an update on the PPC situation," Linda said lowering her voice so Luke couldn't hear.

"Right. Let's talk," Cynthia said gesturing towards the guest room.

"Troy told me they know how Jim died, but they don't know what killed him," Linda whispered even though they were in another room.

"So, how did he die?" Cynthia asked.

"Subdural hematoma."

"Huh?"

"Yeah, that's what I said when Troy told me," Linda said trying not to giggle. "It's basically a severe head injury. Blood collects between the brain and the covering of the brain. It looks like Jim was hit in the head with something. They thought it was likely a rock, but there was a strange mark at Jim's temple."

"Strange in what way?"

"It left an imprint. A tiny outline of a square at Jim's temple. Troy said if Jim had been hit anywhere else but the temple, he'd likely be in the hospital instead of the morgue."

"Really?"

"Seems like either his killer knew what they were doing by targeting his temple or it was a complete fluke accident."

"Jesus. I still don't understand how any of this involves D&A and David. Why would he care what I told the police?"

"I think he just didn't want D&A connected in any way."

"Shit. Just 'cause I found the body doesn't mean I had anything to do with his death."

"You know that, and I know that, but clearly, David doesn't. You did the right thing Cyn. He's just paranoid about his career and how this is all going to affect D&A being in the news like this."

"That doesn't make me feel any better. I need to figure out what David is up to so I can get my job back."

"Do you really want to go back to work there? For that asshole?"

"I like the work and everyone else."

"We'll figure it out. I've got some people looking into David's background and his family."

"David has a family?" Cynthia sounded surprised.

"None of them want anything to do with him. He's been married three times, and apparently, he has a daughter who lives in the city."

"David has a daughter? I can't imagine him having kids."

"He has a son too," Linda added.

"Hey, Linda's on the news." The girls could hear Bob from the other room.

"It's about the other body. I was out at the construction site before I came here." Cynthia and Linda headed to the living room to watch the news. Gayle distracted Luke. She knew it was impossible to anticipate what you would find on the news these days, but it was almost never good. Linda reported the body was well-known activist Kurt Ripple who was a researcher and professor at the university. He had been investigating long-term soil damage as a result of drilling for oil. He was shot in the head, and police believe his death may be connected to Jim's.

"Wow!" Cynthia said. "What's happening to our city?"

"You just haven't been close to it before. This kind of stuff happens all the time, but high-profile oil companies aren't usually the scene of the crime. It's more like back alleys and deserted rundown warehouses."

"You really need to get into a safer line of work. I can't have my best friend in danger every day."

"Oh, please. I'm not in any danger. I'm always there after the fact. Besides, I'd be bored out of my mind if I were in any other line of work. You know that."

"I do," Cynthia said as she snapped off the TV.

30

Not many people were in the office yet. Mostly the audit department. The tax department was starting to get busier but not like the audit department. Their time would come. In just a few short months the roles would be reversed only worse. The office would become a second home to the tax accountants from March until the end of July. Ben hadn't decided if he would continue in the audit department after he passed the final CPA exam. The tax staff seemed to be treated so much better. Audit was where all the students started out. It was the bottom of the totem pole, and the students knew that. It made them work that much harder to get out of audit or move up to audit manager. Most of the managers and partners were good to the students. Most of them except for David.

It was almost 7:45 a.m. and Ben heard David mutter something into his cell phone in a hushed tone as he passed by the bullpen area. David never looked up to see who was working and who he might say good morning to. David didn't care. All he cared about were his clients and making sure they were happy. Ben grabbed his coffee cup and headed towards the staff kitchen area which was also in the direction of David's office. Ben stopped in the kitchen and put his coffee cup on the one-cup brew machine. He selected a cappuccino and pressed the start button. While he was waiting for his drink, he wandered down the hall to see if David had left the door to his office open. It was open enough that Ben could hear David was on his phone.

"I'm not going to lie to you Gord; this looks really bad for PPC. If this project gets shut down, does PPC have enough other work to continue as a viable business?" Of course, Ben couldn't hear what Gord's response was but he was positive PPC had plenty of other projects on the go. They were one of the largest pipeline companies in the country with satellite offices in several other provinces. "Alright. Well, I'll take a look at the numbers and let you know. We may need to add a going concern note to the financial statements if it's probable PPC can't generate sufficient revenue from its other projects. Let me know today if you think of anything else, so we can make any necessary changes and get you the draft statements by the end of the week. I'll check with your lawyers and find out what the potential fees may be around this issue. We'll need to include their legal fees as contingent liabilities."

Ben realized he was so intent on listening in to David's conversation that he hadn't thought about how it would look if a co-worker were to walk by so he casually turned and walked back to the kitchen to check on his cappuccino. Ben grabbed his cup and almost walked straight into Ryan who was dropping off his lunch in the fridge. "Hey, man. What's going on?"

"Ryan! It's about time you showed up," Ben joked. "Almost done with PPC, then on to the next one. Hey, how was your night?"

"I was here pretty late. Grabbed some food on the way home and crashed when I got there."

"Sounds about right." Ben turned and headed back to the bullpen. He stopped and turned back towards Ryan. "Are we still studying tomorrow?"

"Definitely. I need to get back to the books."

"Me too, man."

31

David closed his office door. He had to make a phone call, and although he would have preferred to make it in the privacy of his own home, it had to be done now. Hearing the news about the discovery of another body in connection with PPC made him furious, and he wanted to take his anger out on someone. He paced back and forth in his office while he waited for his cell to connect.

"Are you a fucking idiot?" David hissed into the phone, trying to keep his voice down.

"Well, good morning to you too, sir."

"Don't start with the good morning shit. This is not how this was supposed to go down. I told you to make it look like an accident. Like it was one of his own. And on PPC property? Now it looks like a goddamn revenge killing!"

"Oh relax. You paid me to do a job, and I did it."

"Really? You call that doing your job? You better hope you were smart enough to get rid of the murder weapon because if the rest of the job is as sloppy as the body dump, you'll have the police knocking on your door in no time." David continued to pace.

"Ha! You think I'm dumb enough to do that shit myself? You really have no clue, mister," the voice on the other end of the line laughed mockingly.

"Screw you!" David hung up and tossed his cell phone against the wall before thinking about what he was doing. Jesus. He suddenly felt flushed and had to sit down and take a deep breath to collect himself. He touched his hand to his brow and realized he was sweating. There was a knock outside his door.

"Is everything okay, Mr. Jerew?" Sheryl asked from outside the door. "I was on my way to the kitchen and heard a thump." Sheryl knew David was prone to fits of rage, but they were usually restricted to the verbal variety.

"Everything's fine!" David yelled back. But everything wasn't fine. For once David felt like he had no control over the situation he'd gotten himself into. He opened his top right desk drawer and dug to the bottom. He pulled out an old photograph and stared at it for a few seconds. Although the photo was many years old, just seeing her face calmed David down. He held the photo in his left hand and traced the fingers of his right hand over her face. Soon we'll be together again. Soon you'll see all I've done for you and love me like you did back then.

32

It was a sad day at the university, especially for the environmental scientists. Kurt was such an integral part of their work. Some of Kurt's colleagues were annoyed by how outspoken and rebellious he was, but many more of them appreciated that he stood up for what he believed in and did his best to give a voice to the environment. Many students had already left flowers and pictures outside the building that housed Kurt's office as a way of paying their respects. Eve and some of the other professors in the environmental sciences building decided it was only fitting that someone should stand up for Kurt. Eve would be speaking on the steps of City Hall that afternoon. Several professors and students, as well as other key activists in the city, would be joining her.

Eve wasn't looking forward to seeing April. She knew April and Kurt were close even though she didn't know they were dating. She never knew how to comfort someone when they lost a loved one. To Eve, death was a fact of life, and she treated it as such, rarely shedding a tear over anyone she lost. She had a hard time understanding why people got so emotional about it when she knew it was bound to happen to everyone eventually.

As Eve started down the corridor to her office, she noticed April's door was open, and her light was on. Eve was surprised April was already at work. She assumed April would have been at home preparing for the rally at City Hall. Eve took a deep breath while she tried to come up with the words to express her sympathy to April. "My condolences" sounded too formal and saying "I'm sorry" made it sound like it was her fault. Oh, for crying out loud Eve, just ask her how she's doing.

"Good morning, April. I mean, I'm sorry, I know it's not a good morning. I know you and Kurt were good friends. How are you doing?"

"It's okay, Eve. I've worked for you long enough to know emotions are hard for you."

"You're right. The only thing that makes me emotional is the way people treat our earth, but I do care about you, and Kurt was my friend too. He did so much for this school and helped bring awareness to so many issues in our city."

"You know what, Eve? Kurt would have wanted us to continue to fight, and that's what I'm doing. I wrote a new speech for you last night. I know you said you wanted to avoid drawing attention to PPC, but Kurt was murdered at their construction site. The citizens of our city deserve to know that, and they deserve to know that Kurt did nothing wrong. Kurt's campaigns helped delay the pipeline construction, and if we can delay it even further or even shut it down by drawing attention to his death, I think Kurt would want us to do that."

"I think you're right," Eve replied, shocked at how calm April seemed. "Alright, my dear. Well, I'm going to read this speech you prepared and get myself ready to deliver it."

"You should know that the regulars are planning to be there to back you up. You'll probably have anyone that ever protested alongside Kurt standing behind you on those City Hall steps."

"I was hoping you'd say that. I'll check in with you in about an hour, and we can talk about the logistics."

"Thanks, Eve." April closed her door as Eve headed to her office. She was managing to hold it together for now, but she felt like she was on the verge of a breakdown. She already missed Kurt terribly and had no idea how she was going to go on without him. She slumped down in her chair and turned to face the window. She looked out onto the same parking lot where she had seen the Escalade last night. She thought about the secret that she and Kurt had and how the last time she'd seen him, they argued about it. How she wished she could take back the awful words she said. How she wished she told him she trusted him with all her heart. April didn't know how she was going to keep her secret now that she was the only one who knew.

33

It was almost 11:00 a.m. and Cynthia was busy getting ready to meet Ben for lunch. She felt like she was getting ready for a date, but surely Ben was joking. Why would he be interested in a woman seven years older with a kid? Of course, he was joking, but a little voice in the back of Cynthia's mind wouldn't let it go. What if he did think of her that way? Cynthia decided at the last minute to freshen up her make-up and dress as if she was heading into the office. Cynthia let her mind wander while she applied her lipstick. Ben was adorable with a charming personality to match. Once she was happy that her make-up was perfect, she took a deep breath and let out a big sigh. She hadn't realized she was feeling nervous.

"You look nice, Mommy." Cynthia was so preoccupied she hadn't noticed Luke was watching her from the doorway.

"Thanks, sweetie. You have fun with Grandma and Grandpa while I'm gone, okay." Cynthia said starting down the hall.

"I will."

Cynthia grabbed her car keys and headed out to meet Ben.

The drive downtown couldn't have been smoother. Cynthia wasn't sure how busy traffic would be with it being rush hour, but she made surprisingly good time. She was sure Ben wouldn't be at Scarpino's yet, so she took her time parking. She was happy to find a spot within a few blocks of the deli. A leisurely walk would do her good. Scarpino's was located in the heart of the city's core, just a couple blocks from City Hall which made it a popular lunch spot for employees of neighbouring businesses. Cynthia wondered if David ever lunch had there, but she was pretty sure it wasn't his kind of place.

Cynthia opened the door to Scarpino's and was surprised to see Ben was already waiting for her. He stood up and waved. Cynthia felt a rush of emotions, so many that she wasn't sure exactly what she was feeling, but she knew she had to warn Ben about David. As Cynthia got closer to the table where Ben was, Ben said hi and pulled out a chair for her. Cynthia felt her face flush as she said hi back and thanked Ben for pulling out the chair. She had no idea Ben was such a gentleman. It was something she always admired about Jason.

"How are things at the office today?" Cynthia asked as she sat down.

"Strange, actually. David seems to be freaking out about another dead body relating to PPC."

"Well, it certainly can't be good for them," Cynthia replied. She suddenly felt the overwhelming need to warn Ben.

"Should we order before it gets too busy?" Ben asked.

"Oh, sure."

"It's my treat, remember," Ben said as they walked up to the deli counter. They both ordered pastrami on rye and Cynthia ordered extra pickles. Ben carried the tray of food back to their table.

"Be careful when it comes to David." Cynthia looked around the deli to see if she recognized any of the other patrons. She and Ben were seated at a fairly private booth, but one thing she learned about working with high profile clients was you could never be too careful what you said while out in public.

"Yeah, David is just a high-strung jerk." Ben wanted to call him an asshole, but he didn't feel right about swearing in front of Cynthia.

"I'm not going to argue with you on that, but there's more to it," Cynthia lowered her voice to be extra cautious. "David was following me that night I gave you a ride home."

"What?!" Ben was confused and furious.

"Yeah, you have no idea how happy I was to see you."

"You know, I thought something was up with you, but I just thought you were nervous about having me in the car with your son."

"No, I was freaking out on the inside but trying to cover it up so Luke wouldn't catch on. When I went to pick Luke up from daycare after work, David was there. He threatened my entire family and told me not to say anything more to the police. He told me he would ruin my career too. Then when Luke and I got down to the parkade, David was still there. I just wanted to get out of there, but when I left the parkade, I noticed David was following me."

"What the fuck?" Ben couldn't keep his anger hidden, but he quickly realized what he had said. "I'm sorry, I shouldn't have said that," Ben said, brushing Cynthia's arm with his hand as he said it. Cynthia didn't miss a beat.

"You do know that I've heard the way you and Ryan talk at the office, right? It doesn't bother me." Ben looked embarrassed, and Cynthia thought it was cute. "That's exactly what I thought, by the way. I don't understand what his agenda is or why he didn't want me talking. So, after I told the detective what I saw, David fired me. I'm pretty sure he was following me again or maybe had someone else following me. He sure fired me quickly after I talked to Detective Bain. I think anyone working on this audit should watch their back. At least until I figure out what's going on."

"How are you going to do that? You're not going to confront David, are you?"

"God, no. Linda's helping me dig into David's background, but you didn't hear that from me." Cynthia felt like she could trust Ben.

"I overheard David talking to Gord this morning, but it sounded like the usual audit stuff."

"Will you guys be able to finish the audit this week?"

"I think so. We just need to confirm contingent legal fees and determine if there is a going concern issue then we can wrap up the notes and get a draft out."

"Good. I think it's best for everyone if that job gets wrapped up as soon as possible. There's no telling what David might do now."

34

By the time Ben and Cynthia finished their lunch, the deli was packed, and the downtown core was alive with all kinds of workers on their lunch breaks. Ben insisted on walking Cynthia to her car. As they passed the block where City Hall is located, they heard a voice over a loudspeaker. They looked down the street to see the entire road was blocked by protesters. Cynthia turned down the street to get a better look, and Ben remained right by her side. They looked at each other and Ben raised his eyebrows but didn't say a word.

It was clear the protesters were environmental activists. Many of them had pictures of Kurt on their placards. The crowd was too large for Ben and Cynthia to get to the steps of City Hall, but from where they were standing across the street, they could see that the group had come to remember Kurt and ensure his death wasn't in vain. Dr. Eve Greenwich stood alone at the podium, and there were swarms of activists all around her.

"Approximately four environmental activists in third world countries are killed every week defending their land," came Eve's voice from the loudspeaker.

"Wow, I had no idea," Cynthia uttered as her hand instinctively flattened against her heart.

"Me neither," Ben said as he stood in awe of the crowd and how silently everyone was waiting for Eve's next words.

"But we never expected it to happen in our own country, let alone in the very city we live. We defend our earth because without it we wouldn't exist. We defend it without thinking about the dangers to ourselves, our families, or our friends. Kurt was no different. He was a tireless defender of our prairie lands and accomplished many great things for our city. His research on climate change was among the top in North America, and he contributed to many important global studies. Never once did Kurt stop to think about his own safety."

Cynthia noticed a bit of a ruckus happening at the end of the street. She could still hear Eve talking in the background, but her attention was drawn to the flashing lights that had arrived on the scene. She nudged Ben with her elbow and pointed to the cop cars.

"Shit," said Ben. "You'd think the cops would at least leave them be when they're paying tribute to one of their own." There were at least four police cars at the end of the street now, all with their lights flashing. At least they hadn't turned on their sirens yet. Cynthia glanced towards the other end of the street and noticed that two more cars had formed a blockade at that end, but they didn't have their lights on.

"It's a shame," Eve continued her speech seemingly oblivious to the law's arrival, "that Kurt was struck down in the prime of his career in a place he was fighting its very existence. Yet, I believe, as heartbreaking as it is, he wouldn't have wanted it any other way. Let's remember Kurt today, and always, as we fight to protect our environment." To this, the entire crowd erupted in applause, hoots, and hollers.

"To Kurt!" someone in the crowd shouted and immediately the entire crowd was chanting Kurt's name. Although Cynthia didn't know Kurt, she felt a tear welling up in the corner of her eye. She thought she saw Linda up front and off to the side of the podium. No doubt she was there for the news coverage. Cynthia saw Detective Bain approaching the steps of City Hall. He was having a difficult time navigating his way through the crowd, but that didn't appear to be slowing him down. He was accompanied by two officers in uniform.

"Dr. Eve Greenwich." Eve looked up, shocked the officers would have the nerve to interrupt her tribute to Kurt. April stepped between Eve and Detective Bain.

"Can I help you, officers?"

"Our business is with Dr. Greenwich," Detective Bain replied.

"I'm sure she will be happy to help you once the rally is over," April tried to defer the detective. "We're on public property. We're well within our rights," April continued, noticing the detective wasn't backing down.

"That may be the case, miss, but your supporters are blocking the street, and that wasn't pre-approved." By this time, Eve's attention had turned to the officers. From where Cynthia and Ben stood, they could see Linda and her video crew trying to make their way over to the other side of the crowd where the officers were talking with April and Eve.

"What seems to be the problem, officers?" Eve enquired.

"I'm sorry for your loss, Dr. Greenwich, but I need you to come down to the station with us. You're wanted for questioning in the death of Jim Dunn."

"Can it wait until we're finished here?"

"I'm afraid it can't, and I need you to clear the street." Two more cop cars had arrived as well as a few officers on bicycle. They were making their way through the crowd trying to reopen the street. Eve turned to the crowd with a cold look on her face.

"It seems like these officers don't believe in the freedom of speech or the safety of our city's activists." The crowd went nuts booing and heckling the police.

"I didn't want to do this here or today, doctor, but you've left me no choice. Dr. Eve Greenwich, you have the right to remain silent." Detective Bain continued reading Eve her full Miranda rights while Linda and her crew recorded everything. Ben and Cynthia were still across the street watching everything like it was a dream. They looked at each other, both with the same expression of disbelief.

"You're arresting me for paying tribute to my colleague?" Eve ignored Detective Bain in an attempt to figure out what was going on.

"No, Dr. Greenwich, I'm arresting you for the murder of Jim Dunn."

35

Ben and Cynthia couldn't hear what's going on between Eve and Detective Bain, but it was clear that Eve was being arrested. Ben pulled out his cell phone. "I wonder if Linda is broadcasting live." In a matter of seconds, Ben had the local news station on his phone and was watching the news up close. "It looks like she's being arrested for Jim Dunn's murder." People started to gather around Ben and Cynthia, and they decided it was probably best to move along before things got worse. More police arrived for crowd control, and some of the mob was resistant to move from the street.

Heading back the way they came, Ben and Cynthia weaved in and out of the packed crowd. Ben grabbed Cynthia's hand to make sure they didn't get separated. Cynthia was thankful to have a guide taller than she was to navigate out of the crowd that seemed to be getting angrier by the minute. People were chanting about Kurt and freedom of speech. They didn't seem to understand Eve wasn't being arrested because of the demonstration. Ben and Cynthia made it to the end of the street where some of the activists had started funneling away from City Hall. They had made it out of the main swarm of people and Ben could have let go of Cynthia's hand, but he didn't until they arrived safely at Cynthia's car. Cynthia hadn't even realized she was still holding Ben's hand until he let go.

"So, I guess I'll see you when I see you," Cynthia said awkwardly as she fumbled for her car keys.

"Ryan and I are planning a study session tomorrow after work if you'd like to join us."

"It would be great to get back to some sort of normalcy," Cynthia replied. "I'm meeting Linda, but I can stop by after. But I guess she might be working on this story now. Where are you meeting?"

"We were going to study at D&A but let's meet at the library instead," said Ben, considering Cynthia's recent unemployment.

"Okay, I'll see you tomorrow," Cynthia said getting into her car. Ben waited until Cynthia drove away then walked back to D&A. He wasn't sure what David was up to, but he was sure David better watch his back because he was going to be watching him every step of the way.

Cynthia smiled as she drove back to her parents' house. As much as she didn't want to involve anyone else, she was glad she'd decided to tell Ben about David. She'd hoped he would caution Ryan and Sam as well. At this point, she felt like David was such a loose cannon that anyone who came in contact with him could potentially be in danger. Cynthia arrived at her parents feeling a little more at ease than she had the last few days. Although she wasn't sure how she would be earning a living at this point, she knew she had enough severance pay to last her until after she completed her exam. She was happy to have some extra time to study for the CPA exam, and once she passed, more doors would open for her.

The house was quiet when Cynthia entered through the back door. She was surprised. This was the main entrance and the area of the house where all the action happened since her parents had an open concept floor plan. The TV room and kitchen were at the back entry. Cynthia liked that it was similar to the layout of her place. It made her feel more at home.

"Hello? Anybody home?" Cynthia called.

"Hi, honey," Gayle answered from the front study. Within a few seconds, Gayle appeared in the hallway. "Luke and your dad are just down at the playground." Bob and Gayle's neighbourhood had a vast playground that Luke loved to explore every time they visited. "I was worried about you. Were you trying to call earlier?"

"No, why would you think that?"

"There must have been three hang-ups within an hour. I thought maybe you were having some problems with the payphone since you don't have your cell."

"No. it wasn't me. Were Dad and Luke home when that happened?"

"Yes. It seemed to stop after they left for the playground."

"I don't like the sound of that. I'm going to the playground."

"I'm coming with you," Gayle said as she grabbed her coat. They could have walked, but Cynthia wanted to get to the playground as fast as possible, so they took her car. She'd heard about scammers calling just to find out if anyone was home, but she was more worried that David was checking up on her. He had threatened her family as well as her career, and she wasn't going to take any chances. As the car rounded the bend towards the playground, Cynthia and Gayle saw Luke and Bob walking on the sidewalk, on their way back to the house. Cynthia pulled up next to them and parked the car.

"Mommy!" Luke said excitedly.

"Do you want a ride?" Cynthia asked.

"Let's do it," Bob replied, opening the door for Luke. Cynthia breathed a sigh of relief and realized she was just being paranoid.

36

It was quiet and dark at the PPC offices even though it wasn't quite closing time. Gord had the news playing in the background while he finished up his report for the stakeholders. He was starting to question what David had said about PPC being a going concern and was wondering if they would survive these two murders. The construction site was shut down while Kurt's death was being investigated. Gord and several other PPC employees were wanted for questioning at the police station. Gord had already made an appointment with Detective Bain. He had nothing to hide and no connection to Kurt Ripple.

The footage of Eve's arrest was on again. It had been playing on repeat almost every hour. Gord couldn't help feeling like it was his tip that got her arrested. The news wasn't providing any further details at this point, just that Eve had a reason to kill Jim and the means to do it. Gord couldn't help but feel a little bit shocked. He didn't think his tip would cause Eve to be arrested. He just wanted her to suffer a bit—maybe be questioned and scrutinized. Eve would find that extremely irritating. Never in a million years did Gord think Eve actually killed Jim but it appears he misjudged her. Things became all too clear to Gord now. His affair with Eve was never going anywhere. She was cold and calculating just as she'd been the night she murdered Jim. But how did she do it? Gord just didn't understand.

* * *

Everyone at Bob and Gayle's house was finishing dinner when they heard a knock on the door. It was Linda. She'd come to pick up Cynthia for a shopping date.

"I thought we were going tomorrow," Cynthia said to Linda, surprised that she was standing at the door.

"Yes, that was the plan," said Linda. "But that was before this crazy day and everything that happened this afternoon at Kurt's tribute. "Can you go now?"

"Sure," said Cynthia. She turned to her parents at the table. "Do you mind watching Luke for an hour or two? I should be home in time to put him to bed."

"We don't have anything going on," Bob and Gayle answered, almost in unison.

"Let's go." Cynthia said to Linda with a smile.

"Where do you want to go?" Without waiting for Cynthia to answer, as she often did, Linda added, "I want to check out the shoe sale at The Bay. Looks like you need some new shoes too." Linda glanced at the scuffed up well-worn heels Cynthia was putting on.

"I need to get myself a new cell phone too. Let's head downtown. There's a Bay there and a cell store, I think."

"Cyn, there's a cell store on every block. I don't know why you didn't just ask Ben to grab your phone for you."

"Right! And risk him getting fired too. No, thank you!" Cynthia left Luke and her parents to go shopping with Linda. They decided to take Linda's car downtown rather than the bus, so they could talk about the day's events in private during the drive.

"I just don't get it," Linda said. "Detective Bain said they were arresting Dr. Greenwich because they had motive and a murder weapon. Troy never told me they knew what the murder weapon was."

"Maybe they just figured it out since you saw him," Cynthia said.

"Yeah, I guess. Oh well. So, where should we go first?" asked Linda.

"Do you mind if we stop and get a phone first? I would feel much safer having a cell phone again."

"Did something happen that you're worried about?" asked Linda.

"Not really. My parents got some hang-ups at their house earlier today. I just thought I better not wait too long before getting a cell again. It's nice to have in case of an emergency." After Cynthia took care of buying a new cell phone and setting up her plan, Linda and Cynthia walked to The Bay through the mall. They saw a display in the centre of the mall featuring the big shoe sale The Bay was having and decided to go check it out.

Cynthia loved fancy heels but just couldn't justify buying any tonight. All the shoes she had were good quality and would last her several years, so she really didn't need any. That didn't stop her from trying on a few pairs, though. Linda had already picked out two pairs of fancy heels that were both 75% off. The best friends moved to the boot section where several pairs were half price. Cynthia tried on a pair of spike-heeled boots that went halfway up her thighs. She would never buy a pair of boots like those, but she was having fun pretending.

"Hey, check out my hooker boots," she said to Linda.

"You'd be surprised what some of the interns at work wear," Linda replied laughing.

"We're getting old," Cynthia replied.

"Speak for yourself! Alright, I think I'm done," Linda said, adding a pair of boots to her armload of shoes. "Hard to go wrong at these prices. Did you find anything?"

"Oh, there's some cute shoes for sure, but I don't really need anything."

"Come on, treat yourself."

"I can't. I don't even know when I'll be working again."

"Oh please, you're one of the hardest working, smartest people I know."

"I'll tell you what . . . when I'm back to work, I'll celebrate with a pair of new shoes," Cynthia said, liking the sound of it.

"Deal," Linda said getting in line to pay. Cynthia got in line beside her. "Holy shit!" Linda exclaimed, her gaze fixed on the accessories at the sales counter. She turned to Cynthia, her eyes wide, and whispered so none of the other customers could hear. "I think that's the murder weapon," she said, grabbing a pair of heel protectors from the display. "I've got to get these to Troy."

"What are those?" Cynthia asked.

"One of the best inventions ever! You slip them over your spike heels so you can walk on grass, grates, and gravel, and they also protect your heels from wearing down. Look at the bottom. It's a tiny outline of a square." Cynthia was bewildered looking at the clear heel protectors.

"Well, I guess it doesn't hurt to have Troy take a look."

"This has to be the murder weapon. What else would make a tiny square outline like this? Troy is going to love this!"

37

"I'm going to find you the best lawyer I can, Eve," April said, sitting across from her mentor who was being held in a cell at the Calgary Police Station. This was April's second visit today. She came by earlier today, shortly after Eve was arrested and everyone had dissipated from Kurt's tribute. She had something on her mind she really needed to get off her chest. Kurt would have told her she was crazy, and there was no reason to tell Eve, but that didn't matter now that Kurt was gone.

"We've worked with some amazing environmental lawyers at the university. I'm sure one of their firms must have a trial lawyer who would take my case. I didn't do this, April."

"I know, Eve, I know. I'm going to go straight back to the school and see what I can find out."

"Check my Rolodex. All the lawyers I've worked with will be in there."

"I will. We need to get you out on bail as soon as possible. You don't deserve to be in here. I'm so sorry this is happening to you. Have they given you any details?" April hated seeing Eve sitting in the bare cell in the orange prison jumpsuit. At least she didn't have any roommates yet.

"No, they won't tell me anything until I have a lawyer. All I know is they think I murdered Jim Dunn and apparently they have evidence proving this."

"What evidence?"

"They didn't say."

"Do you want me to call your husband?"

"He was already here. I told him to go home and look after the kids. Try to protect them from the news. For whatever good that will do. I'm sure their classmates will be talking about this tomorrow anyway."

"Eve," April's voice got quiet and shaky. "There's something I need to tell you."

"Party's over ladies." It was Deputy Small coming to let April know visiting hours were over.

"Could we have a few more minutes, please?" April pleaded with the deputy. It took her all day to get the courage to tell Eve her secret, and she didn't want to leave without following through.

"Sorry, miss, no exceptions in the jail," the deputy replied. April stood up and left with the deputy.

"I'll see you as soon as visiting hours start tomorrow and with any luck, I'll have one of the city's top trial lawyers with me." April's eyes filled with tears as she said goodbye to Eve.

"Thank you, April," Eve said, and as she did, April burst into tears and quickly ran out the door.

* * *

The drive back to Bob and Gayle's was a blur. Cynthia was sure Linda broke more than one traffic law on the way, but she wanted to get the heel covers to Troy as fast as possible. He was working the night shift, and Linda texted him to let him know she was going to stop by. The two PPC murders were a priority in the medical examiner's lab.

It was Luke's bedtime, and Cynthia arrived just in time for bath time. Once Luke was in bed, Cynthia sat down with her parents to watch TV. They had waited for the news until Luke wasn't around. S-CAL was showing reruns of Linda's footage of Dr. Greenwich's arrest.

"I just can't believe our famous environmental scientist murdered that accountant," Bob said.

"It does seem a bit ironic with the two of them being on different sides of this pipeline controversy." Gayle took a sip of her tea. "Something Dr. Greenwich said today at the tribute for her colleague really hit me. In other countries, people die every week defending their land. I had no idea. I wonder if they know anything more about Dr. Ripple." Cynthia and her parents watched the rest of the news, but there was no further information about the second murder on PPC's property.

"Cyndi, you know you and Luke are welcome to stay with us as long as you like." Bob sensed Cynthia was a little unnerved.

"Thanks, Dad. It won't be too long. I just need a few days to feel safe on my own again. Losing my job is one thing, but if David were ever to make good on his threats to harm you, or Mom, or Luke, I don't know what I'd do. Being here with you helps me know you're safe."

"You don't need to worry about us, dear."

"I know, Dad. And thanks for letting us stay. It's nice to have some extra company right now." When the news was over, Cynthia grabbed her bag and headed to the spare room where Luke was sound asleep. She pulled out some notes Linda had given her when they were shopping. It was everything she had been able to find out about David so far. Cynthia was surprised at how much information Linda had gathered in such a short amount of time, but she shouldn't have been. Linda was a talented investigative journalist.

The material on David went as far back as his childhood. There was nothing unusual there. The typical stuff. Before David threatened Cynthia, she felt sorry for him and thought he was probably lonely and miserable, but now she realized he was just a cold, heartless man who, no surprise as it turns out, was raised by two cold and heartless parents. David was born and raised on the east coast and came to the prairies after receiving his CPA designation. He was one of the founding partners of D&A which Cynthia used to admire. Now she just wondered how many people he'd threatened to get that position.

There were even notes on David's personal life. He'd had three wives and two children with two of his wives. All three wives had divorced him after only a few years of marriage. His children were both very young the last time he'd seen them. He had a daughter and a son. There wasn't a lot of information about David's kids, just that the daughter would be about Cynthia's age and the son about ten years younger. Cynthia felt a bit of relief for the kids that they hadn't been raised by their father. Maybe they stood a fighting chance of being decent human beings.

As Cynthia flipped through the last few pages of Linda's notes, two things caught her attention. There was a picture of David and Gord James, the CFO of PPC. It looked like they were shaking hands. Cynthia thought it was odd the photo was in the notebook. She made a mental note to ask Linda about it tomorrow. The second thing Cynthia noticed made her realize just how powerful David was—if it was true. He tried to hire a prostitute several years ago shortly after his third marriage ended. It turns out the prostitute was an undercover cop who David paid not to say anything. The cop quit the force shortly after. She left without a word to the department. Cynthia shuddered, wondering if David could have had something to do with the officer's disappearance. She realized David was a man who always got what he wanted and would stop at nothing to make sure that happened. But what did David want now and how was she standing in his way? Cynthia decided to call Linda in the morning and talk it out. They were great at working out puzzles together.

38

It was snowing pretty hard as April pulled up in front of the police station. Eve would be moved to the jail soon, and April wanted to see her and let her know she found a lawyer to take her case. She rushed inside forgetting to pay the parking meter. Visiting hours had just started. After she signed the visitor's log book, April was escorted back to Eve's cell by the guard on duty.

"Jesus Christ, April. You look like shit," Eve said after the guard left them to talk.

"I was up half the night looking for the best lawyer for you. You'd be surprised how many trial lawyers answer their phone in the middle of the night. Do you remember the lawyer that helped our department the last time some university staff got arrested protesting?"

"Yes. Didn't you spend some time in jail that time?"

"Err, yes." April blushed then continued, not wanting to talk about her arrest. "There's a lawyer at his firm who handles murder cases, and he's willing to look at your case."

"Thank god! When do I meet him?"

"This afternoon."

"Do I get to stay here until after I meet with him then?"

"No, you're being transferred to the jail later this morning. Because you've been arrested for murder . . ."

"I can't go to the big jail, April," Eve interrupted frantically. "I won't last there. Don't let them transfer me." Eve started to cry. April had never seen Eve cry before, and she had no idea what to do. She didn't have the heart to tell Eve that the lawyer who would be looking after her case said it could take two or three days before they found out if she would be eligible for bail.

"I'll call your lawyer. Maybe he can stall the transfer or at least come and meet with you sooner so you can find out what evidence they have on you."

"Thank you, April," April said goodbye to Eve and left to make the call to Eve's lawyer. As soon as April got to her car, she dialed Will Bronsky's office.

"Hello, I need to speak to Will Bronsky. It's an emergency."

"One moment please." The voice on the other end sounded so cheerful and efficient. April felt like Eve would be in good hands.

"Will Bronsky."

"Hi, Will. This is April Sundin. I spoke to you last night about Dr. Eve Greenwich's case."

"Yes, of course."

"Does Eve have to be moved to the jail so soon? She's a wreck and says she'll never last there. Is there any way you can do something to have her detained here at the police station holding cell a little longer? Until we find out about her bail?" April pleaded with the lawyer.

"I'm afraid it doesn't look good, April. Some information was leaked this morning. I haven't been able to confirm with the police yet, but it looks like Dr. Greenwich was being blackmailed by the deceased. The police also believe they found the murder weapon in Dr. Greenwich's home. A high heel with a heel protector of all things." April thought about the heels stashed under her desk wondering if Eve had borrowed them.

"Shit!" April whispered into the phone, not realizing Will could hear her.

"I'm sorry, what was that?" Will asked.

"Oh, nothing, I'm sorry. I've got to go." April hung up. The news about the evidence made her feel sick to her stomach, and she was as white as a ghost. She knew what she had to do. She just hoped it wasn't too late and that Eve would be alright for the next twenty-four hours.

* * *

What the hell are you doing, April? David wondered as he watched April pull away from the police station. He followed her to the school where she parked her car and headed into the lab. She was acting like it was business as usual, but David had been following her for long enough to know this wasn't her regular pattern of behaviour on a weekday morning. David feared April was about to do something stupid and he had to stop her. He put on a ball cap and sunglasses, hoping to blend in with the university students. He wasn't sure exactly where he was going to find the information he needed, but he figured he could start at April's office. As he got close to her office, he could hear her rummaging around. It sounded like she was pacing back and forth in her office talking to herself. He heard her dial a phone number.

"Will Bronsky, please." There was a pause. "Thank you," David heard April say. "Hi, Mr. Bronsky. It's April Sundin again. I'm sorry I cut you off before. Can you meet me at the police station?" There was another pause while Will replied to April. David had no idea who Will Bronsky was, but he didn't like the sound of this one-sided conversation. "No, it's not about Eve. I need your help. I would prefer if you could meet me at the station. Eve didn't kill Jim Dunn. I did."

David couldn't believe what he was hearing. April was about to spill the secret he'd been working so hard to keep for her. He turned around and high-tailed it to his Escalade as quickly as he could. He knew April would be right behind him and he couldn't risk being spotted.

Miraculously, David made it back to his vehicle without drawing any suspicion to himself. He had started the vehicle with its remote starter as he exited the building. As soon as he jumped in, he was mobile. He waited until he turned onto

Crowchild Pass to feel under his seat. He breathed a sigh of relief realizing that his 22-calibre Ruger was tucked safely in its default position.

39

The weather could be better, Cynthia thought as she looked out the window at the snow which seemed to be falling even heavier now than it was just an hour ago when she woke up. The snow always reminded her of Jason. In the first few months after Jason's death, it always made her sad, but she learned to look at it as a reminder that Jason was always with her. Cynthia texted Linda as soon as she got up, knowing that she would already be hard at work on one of the two murders she was covering. She didn't like bothering her when she was so busy, but Cynthia had some questions about the research Linda gave her regarding David. Cynthia was hopeful they could at least meet for a quick lunch. Cynthia's cell phone pinged with the answer.

I'm swamped but come to my office for lunch. We can talk then.
Thank you! Cynthia texted back. *I'll bring lunch. Any requests?*
Surprise me.

For Cynthia, someone who packed a lunch for work almost every day, two lunches out in two days felt extravagant, but she was excited to find out the answers to her questions. She sat down on her parents' couch to read some of the books Luke had piled up on the coffee table. Cynthia was enjoying not having to rush off to work first thing in the mornings. She could tell Luke liked the extra attention too. They enjoyed their morning together reading books and doing crafts with Gayle.

* * *

"Is there any way you can get the undercover cop's phone number?" Cynthia asked Linda. They were tucked away in Linda's private office eating the takeout sushi Cynthia brought for lunch.

"I think my source can get it. Actually, I'm positive he can. I'm just not sure she'll be interested in talking. That was seven years ago."

"I know, I just feel like she might know something about David. She had to be pretty scared to just disappear."

"Or embarrassed to be paid off like that. Cops taking bribes isn't pretty," Linda replied. "Let me see what I can find out." The sushi was almost gone, and Linda needed to get back to the Kurt Ripple story, but Cynthia had one more question for her friend.

"What's with the picture of David and Gord shaking hands? I didn't see why that was so significant. PPC is David's client, and Gord is their CFO. Seems pretty normal that they'd be shaking hands."

"How closely did you look at the picture?"

"Probably not as close as you, my eagle-eyed friend," Cynthia said laughing a little.

"Here," Linda handed Cynthia a magnifying glass. Cynthia took another look at the photo through the lens.

"I don't get it. What am I looking for?" Cynthia still didn't see the significance of the image.

"Look at their hands. The handshake. Notice anything?"

"Is that . . .? It looks like a piece of paper between their hands."

"Bingo! My guess is it isn't a piece of paper. I think it's an envelope, but we reporters must stick to the facts, so I've got someone checking into it. I have to tell you with this guy and knowing how he's treated you, it's reeeaaally hard to stick to the facts." Linda let her eyes roll back in her head as she said it as if she was trying to contain her anger towards David.

"But if that's an envelope, that could mean cash exchanged hands. I wonder if that's why David's acting so paranoid? He was protecting Gord. But why did Gord say he found the body?

Who was he protecting?" Cynthia said half to herself and half to Linda. Linda's cell phone beeped just as she swallowed the last of her sushi and took a big swig from her water bottle.

"That's one of my sources. Something's going down at the police station. I gotta go. I'll keep you posted, and if I can get that number, I'll text you later."

"Okay, thanks. I better get back to Luke. Careful on the roads."

"Don't worry; I think I'm going to need my camera crew. We'll be in the van which is awesome in the snow." Cynthia felt only a little better hearing this. She knew Linda's crews didn't pay much attention to the speed limit when they were chasing a story. Cynthia headed out right behind Linda, but she would be driving much slower back to her parents. She knew there was no sense taking risks on the winter roads and the snow hadn't stopped all morning.

40

The drive to Bob and Gayle's took about 45 minutes, twice as long as it usually would. Linda's office was in the southwest area of the city, and Bob and Gayle were a little south of downtown. Cynthia turned down the street and noticed a black Escalade in their driveway. At first, she tried to figure out who was visiting her parents, but then the words registered in her brain. Black Escalade. Cynthia's heart immediately started racing as she imagined all the possible scenarios that could be playing out, all the possible ways David was making good on his threat to hurt her family.

She jumped out of her car, not stopping to close the door behind her. She raced into the house, and there he was, David Jerew, sitting at the kitchen table with Luke and her parents. There was a gun with a silencer on the table, and David was resting his hand on it. Cynthia froze.

"Hello, Cynthia," David said barely giving Cynthia a chance to register what was happening.

"David, you can't do this," Cynthia tried to reason with him, tears already streaming down her cheeks. Luke was sitting next to David.

"Mommy!" Luke cried. Cynthia ran over to Luke, bent down and picked him up out of the chair he was sitting in.

"Put him down!" David yelled. "You don't get to hug your son anymore. Say goodbye, Ms. Webber. Luke is coming with me."

"Never," Cynthia said. "You can't take him!" Cynthia could barely see her eyes were so blurry from the tears. She put Luke down and tried to focus, tried to come up with a plan to outsmart David. Gayle was sitting across from Luke, and her dad was across from David with his back to the door where Cynthia had arrived. David lifted the gun off the table and pointed it at Cynthia as he stood up.

"You couldn't just leave well enough alone. You had to go tell the police that you found that earring. Well, now my little goody-two-shoes daughter has gone and turned herself in for Jim's murder. You will find a way to get her out of jail, or you'll never see your son again. An eye for an eye, Ms. Webber." David said, not realizing Cynthia had nothing to do with April turning herself in. He was angry and needed an outlet.

"How am I going to do that?" Cynthia sobbed.

"I don't care if you have to confess to the murder yourself," David retorted. "Get my April out of jail. You have two days to do it." David grabbed Luke by the arm as Luke started hitting him with his free hand.

"No, baby, you'll only make it worse," Cynthia tried to calm Luke. She didn't want David shooting him because he was pissed off. "I'll come get you as soon as I can." Cynthia took a deep breath as David and Luke walked by her. All she wanted to do was throw herself on David and rip Luke away from him, but David had his gun trained on Cynthia. As David reached for the door, Bob jumped up from his chair and launched himself at David, at the same time breaking David's hold on Luke. Luke ran to Cynthia and Cynthia wrapped him in her arms and hung on tight as she screamed for Bob.

"Dad!"

The impact of Bob throwing himself at David forced David back towards the couch in the living room. He bounced off the couch and back towards Bob while Gayle, Cynthia, and Luke looked on in disbelief. Bob had knocked a lamp off one of the end tables that was placed near the living room window.

"Is that how you want to play it, old man?" David said aiming his Ruger at Bob. Bob grabbed the lamp from the floor and stepped towards David swinging overhead meaning to come down with a sharp blow, but as he raised the lamp, David fired his gun.

Bob instantly fell to the ground and let out a wail. He was on his right side in the fetal position facing David, clutching his chest with his left arm. Blood was quickly soaking through his shirt.

"Bob!" Gayle screeched running over to her husband and kneeling at his side.

"Get away from him," David warned.

"No!" Gayle cried.

"Go on, Gayle, I'm okay," Bob moaned.

"You're coming with me, old man. On your feet," David ordered.

"He needs medical attention," Gayle yelled at David, still not willing to leave Bob's side.

"I'm warning you, get out of my way." David was walking towards Bob who was trying to stand. His left hand was soaked with blood and still on his chest about halfway between his heart and his shoulder where the bullet had entered his body. All the colour had drained out of his face. Gayle, Cynthia, and Luke were all full-on bawling. Cynthia was trying to think of a way to get to the phone and call 9-1-1 without David noticing. Bob was on his feet, bent over at the waist. He winced as David grabbed his right arm just above the elbow. David and Bob were at the door. David was pointing his gun at Gayle who just wouldn't let Bob go.

"It's alright, Gayle," Bob said in a whisper. "It's all going to be alright." Gayle just sobbed in response.

Cynthia started inching her way further into the kitchen where the nearest phone was. She had dropped her bag at the door when she first arrived, so her cell phone was all the way across the room.

"Don't you think of calling the cops, now," David said as if reading Cynthia's mind. "Your job is to free my April. I want her out of jail by Sunday. When she's free and clear, I'll take pops here to the hospital. Not a minute sooner."

"How do we know he's not going to die in the meantime," Gayle shrieked through blubbering cries.

"Don't you worry about that. Old Bob's not going to die on my watch. He's not going to be too comfortable, but as long as Cynthia holds up her end of the bargain, Bob will live to a ripe old age." David turned his back to drag Bob into the driveway where his Escalade was parked. Cynthia picked up Luke and followed Gayle out the door. Bob was staggering sideways as David dragged him by his right arm. With his left hand, Bob reached up and deliberately touched the top of his head while looking at Cynthia.

"Remember Colorado, Cyndi?" Cynthia thought the gunshot wound must have made Bob delirious.

"What are you talking about, Bob?" Gayle sobbed uncontrollably as David forced Bob into his Escalade.

"Colorado," Bob mouthed and tried to pat his head again. Gayle looked at Cynthia. Cynthia's expression changed from desperation to hope as she grabbed Gayle's arm and tried to guide her back into the house. Gayle wouldn't go until she could no longer see the tail lights of David's Escalade. Cynthia managed to get Gayle in the house and sitting in a chair. Luke stood next to Gayle, petting her back like she was his cat. Nobody spoke. Cynthia ran to the phone and started dialing 9-1-1.

"No, Cyndi, you heard David. No cops."

"Trust me, Mom. We need their help. If we do what David says, we're just playing his game. Plus . . . Colorado."

"What do you mean Colorado? You and your dad don't make any sense."

"It makes perfect sense. Dad was giving us a message. Remember when we took that trip to Colorado when I was about nine or ten? I asked Dad why the bikers always waved at each other by pointing down at the ground and then a couple of times we came across some speed traps. Dad told me to watch the bikers in front of us warn the other bikers about the speed trap. They tapped their heads with their left hands. Dad was telling us to call the cops! He can handle himself, Mom. I know it looks bad, but we need to trust that calling the police is the right thing to do." Gayle seemed to calm down a little hearing this. She turned to Luke and gave him a big hug.

"I'm so sorry you had to go through that, sweetie. Grandpa's going to be alright." Cynthia had connected with 9-1-1 and was reporting the incident. Five minutes later, a news van pulled up in Gayle and Bob's driveway. It was Linda. She got out with one of her cameramen and told the rest of her crew she'd meet them at the office.

"Oh my god, are you okay?" she asked Gayle and Luke. Cynthia lifted her hand from across the table as if to wave at her friend.

"How did you know?" Gayle asked.

"We heard it on the police scanner after we left the station. We've got some drones at the station. I made a call on our way here. They'll be up in the sky right away. We should be able to figure out where David's taking Bob."

41

Just a few hours ago, their positions were reversed. Eve was in jail and April was visiting, trying to figure out how she could help her friend and mentor. April knew she'd done the right thing. It was her fault Jim Dunn was dead. She'd gone to PPC's office that night to meet Kurt and convince him to come to the university benefit with her. Kurt hadn't wanted their relationship to be public just yet. April was dressed up and wearing the cute heels that Eve borrowed and left at her house to be discovered by the police.

Everything started out fine at PPC. Her friends were protesting the pipeline and trying to get Jim riled up. She couldn't figure out why on earth Kurt had planned a protest for that time of the night, but when she got there, she realized Kurt and the other protesters had been drinking. Everything seems like a good idea when you're drinking. April was just going to leave and attend the benefit as planned, but Jim had to go and open his rude mouth. The way he talked to her friends was appalling. Then he came outside and started yelling at them some more. Her friends were throwing rocks at Jim like they were participating in a barbarian stoning ritual. Before she had a chance to think about the potential danger of the situation, she took off one of her heels and threw it at Jim as hard as she could. She thought a shoe would do a lot less damage than a rock. She wasn't expecting to hit him, but she was wrong.

Jim dropped to the ground instantly. April wanted to call

9-1-1 right then and there, but Kurt told her to go to her benefit, and he would call 9-1-1 after she left. She didn't realize Kurt was going to leave Jim in a pipe to die. Eve listened empathetically as April finished telling her story for the second time in about as many hours.

"I'm so sorry, Eve. I didn't mean to cause you any harm," April apologized with tears in her eyes. Eve wasn't sure what to think of all this. She stood up. The empathy had turned to anger. Eve turned to April. Her face was scarlet, and her hands were balled into fists.

"You let me sit here. You let people believe I'm a murderer."

"I'm sorry, Eve. I tried to tell you yesterday. I'm so sorry," April said sobbing. Eve simply turned and walked away.

* * *

Back at Bob and Gayle's, Linda was arranging for the drones to be sent into the sky. The station owned four and Linda wanted them all activated. She explained to Gayle and Cynthia that there was no way she could keep this story out of the news, but she would try and be as gentle on the family as she could and delay their interview as long as possible. In the living room, Linda's cameraman tried to distract Luke with a video on his cell phone. The police had come and gone. They had questioned Cynthia, Gayle, and Luke about the incident and were prepared to start searching for Bob immediately. The police asked Linda to let them know if the drones discovered anything.

Gayle was beside herself with worry, and Cynthia suggested she take a nap and try to relax. Linda motioned for Cynthia to follow her to the spare room so they could talk in private.

"I'm sorry, Cyn, I know you have a lot to process right now. My assistant found the undercover cop who David bribed. She's in Denver. Layla's trying to get in touch with her now. If she does, I want to interview her myself and see if she'd be willing to come forward in light of everything that's happened involving David."

"That's such good news." Cynthia was relieved and surprisingly calm given the circumstances.

42

She didn't know where else to go. Her husband had practically disowned her in the short time she was in jail. Eve stood on the front steps of Gord's condo looking up at the street lights noticing how pretty they looked with the snow floating through the glow of their light. Gord opened the door.

"I thought you were in jail?" he said letting his jaw gape a little. He wasn't sure if he should be scared or relieved. Did Eve know he tipped the cops? Did she really kill Jim? How is she free right now?

"Can I come in?"

"I don't know, Eve; I thought you were done with me."

"You're right but, I don't have anywhere else to go, Gord. I'm not welcome at my house. My husband believes the news. He thinks I murdered Jim even though April confessed hours ago. Did you hear?"

"What? April confessed? Did she do it?"

"She did it." Eve raised her eyebrows and her volume. "Why would she turn herself in if she didn't do it? Come on. Are you going to let me in or what?"

"Yeah, you can come in but don't get any ideas. This isn't a booty call." Gord turned his back on the door, grabbed the remote off the couch, and turned off the movie he was watching. The only other light in the condo was coming from over the stove. That didn't stop Eve from noticing a glass of bourbon and half-eaten takeout on the coffee table.

"Since when do you watch movies?"

"I just needed an escape, you know. Besides, I watch movies. We were always too busy sneaking around to just enjoy each other's company and watch movies." Gord felt relieved. He could tell from Eve's tone that she was in a decent mood. That would not be the case if she knew he had turned her in.

"Let's watch one now," Eve said, suddenly wanting to forget everything that had happened in the last couple of days.

"Sit down," Gord said, feeling a little more like a welcoming host. "You want a drink?"

"You better believe I do." Eve made herself comfortable on the couch while Gord poured her a Bacardi and orange juice.

"Here you go," Gord said, joining Eve on the couch. Eve had already turned the movie back on. Gord couldn't help thinking how beautiful Eve looked sitting there in the dim light.

"Thank you," Eve said, taking the drink and guzzling half of it in one gulp. She set it down on the coffee table as Gord tried to sit down next to her. Eve grabbed his arms while she laid back on the couch, so Gord had no choice but to lay on top of her missionary style. "Make love to me," she whispered in Gord's ear then gave it a nibble for old times' sake. Gord was happy to oblige.

43

She didn't want to make the call, but she didn't know who else to turn to. Cynthia waited while the phone connected.

"Hello?"

"Hi, Ben. It's Cynthia."

"Cynthia, how are you? I tried to call earlier. I saw the news about your dad. Are you okay? If you're calling to cancel studying tonight, don't even worry about it."

"Actually, I am strangely okay. I guess after you find a dead body, you come to expect the unexpected. My mom's taking it pretty hard though. That's actually why I'm calling. I need to ask a favour." Cynthia hesitated a little.

"Anything." Ben was eager to help.

"Would you mind keeping my mom and Luke company for a couple of hours? I want to help Linda monitor the drones in the newsroom. They are graciously letting us use them to try and figure out where David's hiding my dad."

"Yes, of course. I'll be right over."

"Thank you. I just didn't feel right about leaving them here alone. My mom is still pretty on edge. I think it will help if you're here."

"I'll see you soon," Ben said. Cynthia said goodbye to Ben and hung up. She looked towards the living room where Luke and Gayle were watching cartoons. The silliness will do them both some good, Cynthia thought.

"Mom, I'm going to meet Linda and see if the drones have any leads yet. Now that it's dark, the police think David may try and move Dad from wherever he's been hiding him. I asked Ben to come and stay with you and Luke while I'm gone. I'll only be a couple of hours."

"That's fine, Cyndi. Thank you. I'll feel much better with Ben here. He seems like such a nice boy."

"Yes, you keep saying that Mom. He's hardly a boy anymore, but yes, he is nice." Cynthia walked around to the front of the couch and sat down next to Luke. "Did you hear that, bud? Ben is coming over to keep you and Grandma company for a little while. I'm going to go see if I can help Linda find Grandpa."

"Okay, Mommy." Luke leaned into Cynthia and gave her a big bear hug. Cynthia didn't want to leave, but she knew Gayle and Luke would be safe with Ben, not to mention the undercover cops who were monitoring the house. After Cynthia had called 9-1-1 that morning, Linda had gone with her to the police station where they met with Detective Bain, and Cynthia gave as many details about the incident as she could remember. Detective Bain insisted three undercover cops be assigned to Gayle, Cynthia, and Luke in case David came after them again.

Cynthia heard a quiet knock on the door. She could see Ben's car through the kitchen window.

"Hi," she said almost blushing. She had never seen Ben in jeans before. She always saw him at the office, or as he was coming or going from it, so he was always in his business clothes. He looked good. Cynthia found herself fighting the urge to hug him. She was so grateful to him for staying with her family. She also wondered if he smelled as good as he looked.

"Are you okay?" Ben asked.

"Uh, yeah. Sorry, just distracted."

"That's understandable. Are you okay to drive to the newsroom by yourself?" Ben asked, concerned.

"Oh, I won't be by myself. I'll have a tail. See that car?"

Cynthia said pointing across the street to the neighbour's driveway. "There's a cop in there. Each of us has one assigned to follow us until my dad is found and David is in custody."

"Good," Ben said, seeming relieved.

"Well, I should get going. I am sorry about tonight. I was looking forward to a quiet night studying. I'll be back as soon as I can." Ben always admired Cynthia's ability to remain calm under pressure, but she seemed unusually so tonight. He was worried about her but covered it up.

"Take your time and don't worry about the studying. There will be plenty more opportunities for that," Ben said with a wink and a charming smile.

44

Linda was finishing a snack when Cynthia texted her. It was after hours, and the news station was closed to the public, so Linda had to meet Cynthia at the front door.

"Come in," Linda said as she opened the door for Cynthia. "I've got some news about David. We were able to track down the ex-cop he bribed years ago. At first, she didn't want to talk, but then she told me to give her a few hours, and she would call me back with some information that might help your situation."

"That's amazing. How's it going with the drones?"

"It turns out there are a lot of black Escalades in the city. We've been concentrating the search on the areas where David is known to frequent—the office, clients' offices, his home, co-workers. So far there hasn't been a lot of hits, but Detective Bain thinks he will make his move in the dark if he's going to move at all." Linda paused and looked at her notes. "Her name is Katrina Wilde. She lives in Denver now."

"Really?" Cynthia asked in disbelief.

"Yeah, why?"

"Nothing really. When my dad was signalling to call the cops, it was because of a trip through Denver that I knew what he was trying to tell me."

"Crazy," Linda replied, preoccupied with the video footage from the drones.

"This whole thing is crazy." Cynthia started to lose the hope she'd had all day. She looked up at the video footage from the drone that was monitoring the area around the PPC construction site. "Do you see that?"

"Where?"

"It looks like something's headed towards the PPC construction site," Cynthia said, pointing at the screen. It was too dark to tell the colour of the vehicle, but Cynthia and Linda could definitely make out headlights on the construction site property which was supposed to be shut down. Cynthia pulled out her cell phone to call Detective Bain. "Whether or not that's David, I'm sure the detective would want to know someone's at the construction site."

"Especially in the dark," Linda replied in support. Linda watched the screen while Cynthia talked to Detective Bain. The vehicle stopped moving, and the lights turned off. As if reading Linda's mind, Calvin, the drone operator, switched the drone's camera to infrared mode.

"What's going on?" Cynthia asked, returning from her call with the detective.

"The vehicle stopped in front of some equipment. With the lights off, it's hard to see what's going on out there. Apparently, Calvin and I have a telepathic connection. He switched to infrared mode. The camera senses heat so if anyone gets out of the vehicle, we should see yellow blobs moving around. That large yellow blob is the vehicle."

"Detective Bain's going to send a patrol car out to the construction site right away," Cynthia said, hopeful that Detective Bain would find her dad. Cynthia and Linda watched the screen attentively. Linda nudged Cynthia when she saw a yellow blob get out of the driver's side.

"Look, there's the driver," Linda said enthusiastically.

"Can't they get any closer? Maybe we could make out some facial features."

"No, we can't risk them seeing the drone and taking off. I'd be surprised if they haven't heard it already." Cynthia and Linda watched as the yellow blob wandered further into the construction site. They watched the blob walk around for several minutes and then get back into the vehicle. Another vehicle approached the construction site.

"Do you think that's the police already?"

"It could be. It's hard to tell with the infrared on. Let me see if the operator can switch it back to the regular camera. If it's the cops, we should be able to see the flashing lights." Before Linda finished texting Calvin, he had already switched the camera on the drone.

"Where is he?" Cynthia asked. "It's like he can see and hear us."

"He's on the roof so I'm pretty sure he can't hear us. The drone can fly up to 30 miles away from the controller, so we're still within range of the construction site. It's pretty crazy." The other two operators are at different locations to make sure there isn't any interference between the three drones."

"Look," Cynthia said, interrupting her friend and pointing at the screen. "It is the cops, and I don't know if it's just wishful thinking, but that does look an awful lot like a black Escalade." The pair watched as the officer got out of his vehicle and walked over to the driver's side of the Escalade. He remained there for a few minutes then got back in his cruiser while the Escalade drove off. Cynthia and Linda looked at each other disheartened.

45

From where he was positioned on the floor, Bob could see flashes of red and blue coming in through the window of the foreman's trailer. David had left him there after he took him from his home. Bob was positive Cynthia had called the police as he signaled. So far David was making good on his promise to keep Bob alive. He'd bandaged Bob up enough to slow the bleeding. The bullet had gone through just under Bob's shoulder. He was still in a lot of pain, and all he wanted to do was go to sleep. Even in the rough state as he was in, Bob still managed to laugh to himself when someone, he assumed was David, arrived with a bag of fast food, opened the trailer door and tossed it in like Bob was some kind of wild animal. The last thing on Bob's mind was food. He had been forcing himself to drink the water David left behind earlier. He knew keeping his fluid intake up would help him get through this. He also knew he couldn't just sit there propped up against the trailer wall. He had to find a way to get that cop's attention.

Thankfully, David hadn't tied Bob's hands together, but his ankles were bound together with a zip strip. Bob tried to bring himself to stand so he could open the window and call to the officer. He managed to get to his knees but didn't have the strength or coordination to stand on his feet to get to the window. Maybe he should eat some of that food, after all, to keep his strength up. The smell of it made his stomach turn. He looked up towards the window to see the flashes of red and blue light were gone. His heart sank a little as he realized the police had left the construction site. He hoped they had left with David in custody.

Lucky for Bob, the foreman's trailer was small. Bob laid down again and was trying to crawl to the bag of food while being sure to avoid using his injured shoulder. The smell of the food only made Bob more nauseous the closer he got to it. But he felt like it was his only option if he was going to keep his energy up, so once he reached the bag, he forced himself to take a few bites of the burger. As he ate, he looked around the trailer for something to free his legs from the zip strip. There were several drawers in the kitchen area of the trailer. Bob was determined to look in them. Surely David wouldn't have been so sloppy as to leave a knife behind, but Bob had to look anyway.

Bob set the remaining burger aside, feeling like that was all he could handle for now. He shimmied on his butt over to the kitchen area smiling as he remembered a game he used to play with Luke where they pretended they were trains by using a similar motion. Bob opened the lower drawers and peeked in, hoping to find some sort of tool that could help him. The drawers mostly contained napkins and paper plates. He found a tattered pocketbook in another. The last drawer was above Bob's head, so he had to feel his way around it. It felt like it contained more napkins, but Bob pushed them aside holding his breath that there would be something helpful hiding underneath. In a sudden surprised motion, he jerked his hand back out of the drawer.

46

The city lights were hard on Cynthia's eyes as she drove back to Bob and Gayle's from S-CAL. Her mind was occupied with how she was going to free April from jail by Sunday. Linda had filled her in on April's confession which was now one of the city's top news stories. Jim's death had been an accident, but April would still be facing manslaughter charges. Cynthia wished she could just pay to bail April out, but she didn't have that kind of money. Maybe Gayle could help her get the money? Technically, it would satisfy David's demands, and April would be free on bail. Cynthia made a mental note to bring it up to her mom.

As Cynthia pulled in to the driveway, she hardly felt tired at all. The adrenaline from the day's events had her wired. She parked beside Ben's car and realized she'd forgotten all about the favour she'd asked of him. It was past 10 p.m., and Cynthia felt guilty she'd taken longer than she'd planned. The house was dimly lit inside, so she quietly snuck in and closed the door behind her. To her surprise, Ben was asleep on the couch. His laptop was open on the coffee table, and one of his textbooks rested next to it. Cynthia wasn't sure if she should wake him or not. She knew he would have to get up early for work in the morning.

There was a folded blanket on a recliner that faced the coffee table. Cynthia grabbed it and carefully draped it over Ben. Just as she was placing the final edge of the blanket across Ben's shoulders, he opened his eyes.

"Hey," he whispered as if they'd been friends forever.

"I'm sorry it's so late," Cynthia whispered back, careful not to wake Luke or Gayle. Ben sat up holding the blanket around himself.

"Thanks," he said, looking at the blanket. "It's no problem. I'm usually up a lot later. I guess I was just tired. I had fun hanging out with your mom and Luke."

"Well, I'm sure they appreciated the company, and I definitely appreciate you coming over."

"There's something I wanted to talk to you about." Ben looked at Cynthia, and she felt nervous wondering if the "something" had to do with their non-date. "If you want me to stay out of it, just let me know, but something didn't sit right with me about the PPC audit. Ryan and I found some cash transactions in the shareholder loan accounts that weren't explained. Sam said he was going to ask the client about it, but there aren't any notes indicating that he signed off on it. Instead, there's a note from David. I know we were rushing to finish with everything that's going on right now but . . . something just didn't feel right."

"What does it say?" Cynthia was a little disappointed Ben wanted to talk about work, but she was excited he might be onto something.

"Not material. That was it. And I feel like maybe I wasn't supposed to see that. I only went back to check because of the trouble that PPC's been in with the murders. I was wondering if any notes had been added about their going concern status. The file's already been locked down, and the audit's been finalized, but something doesn't sit well with me. Here, let me show you." Ben opened his laptop and logged into the D&A virtual private network (VPN). He looked at Cynthia while he waited for his laptop to complete the login process. Cynthia could feel Ben looking at her. She wanted to look into his kind eyes but resisted. She was still feeling bad for calling him a frat boy just a few days ago.

Ben was into the VPN. He opened PPC's file so he could show Cynthia David's note. "You have more audit experience than I do, but shouldn't there be a little more documentation?"

"Absolutely. PPC is still a private company. Generally, shareholder loan transactions like this would be discussed with the client, and the reason for the withdrawal of funds would be documented. Here, like this one," Cynthia said, taking control of Ben's laptop. "See how each line item is clearly explained whether it's going in or out of the shareholder's loan account."

"Yeah, I thought this might be bad."

"It really only puts David on the line because he's the one who signed off on it, but it seems like the questions you had about it have been deleted from the file which isn't great. Shit!" Cynthia exclaimed remembering the file Linda have given her about David. She pulled it out, wondering if it was a good idea to share it with Ben. She'd told him everything else so why not this too? "You have to swear to keep what I'm about to show you, between us."

"Of course," Ben said, nodding with wide eyes.

"When David fired me, I asked Linda to see what she could find out about him. This is the file she gave me. Check this out," she said flipping to the photo of David and Gord shaking hands.

"Is that an envelope?" Ben said pointing to what was being exchanged between Gord and David.

"Yes. And Linda found an ex-undercover cop that David bribed several years ago to keep quiet about him trying to hire her to have sex with him."

"No way!" Ben looked disgusted. "I can't believe I once looked up to that guy. Kind of makes you wonder if he's just bought his way to the top."

"I need to find out why this much cash was transferred out of the shareholder's loan," Cynthia said pointing to the unexplained $10,000 transaction.

"I'll help. What do you want me to do?" Ben said excitedly.

"Nothing. You still work at D&A, remember. I don't want you putting your career in jeopardy. You've done nothing wrong, but if David finds out you're digging into this, who knows what will happen. Hell, he'll probably fire you if he finds out we're friends."

"Good point. Let me at least print this page for you. If you need me to get anything from D&A, let me know."

"Thanks. I'll see if I can talk to these shareholders tomorrow. Looks like a husband and wife from the names on the account." Cynthia pointed at the screen that Ben had just sent to print on the printer that was set up in the spare room.

"Your mom said it was okay that I used her printer," Ben said, looking at Cynthia while covering his mouth to yawn. Maybe frat boys are okay after all, Cynthia thought to herself as Ben packed up his laptop and textbooks and flung his backpack over his shoulder. Cynthia walked Ben to the door. "Let me know how it goes tomorrow. I'll worry about you if I don't hear from you at some point. And, I hope you find your dad soon." Before Cynthia could say anything in response, Ben turned back to Cynthia, ran his finger along her jawline and gave her a soft peck on the cheek. "I'll talk to you tomorrow," he said and turned to walk to his car.

Cynthia stood in the doorway with her hand on her cheek staring at Ben for what seemed like an inappropriate amount of time. Then she turned towards the door and closed it behind her, a smile creeping across her face. A buzzing noise coming from her purse jolted Cynthia back to reality. It was her cell phone.

"Hello?" Cynthia answered in a hushed voice, careful not to wake her mom or Luke.

"Hi, Cynthia. It's Detective Bain. We located Mr. Jerew's black Escalade at the PPC construction site, but the driver said some guy paid him to drive the Escalade out there. The site has been shut down while we investigate Kurt Ripple's murder. The crime scene tape didn't appear to be tampered with, but I'll send a cruiser out in the morning to take another look around."

"Thank you, Detective. I appreciate the update," Cynthia hung up feeling a little disappointed. She was sure David was driving that Escalade. If Gayle had the money to bail April out of jail, that was their next best hope for seeing her dad again.

47

The morning sun glistened through Gord's bedroom window, landing on Eve's cheek. She blinked her eyes awake taking a moment to realize where she was. She'd had a few more drinks than she'd planned last night and wasn't ready to wake up. Not knowing what time it was, she felt an urgency to call Will Bronsky and find out if April was eligible for bail. Although Eve was still upset with April, she had set plans in motion yesterday shortly after she was released that would guarantee the money would be available for bail if needed.

"Good morning," Gord whispered in Eve's ear giving it a little nibble, hoping for a replay of last night's action. Eve sat up, pushing Gord away as she did.

"I need to get home and shower while everyone is gone for the day," she said, jumping out of bed and searching for her clothes which she quickly realized were downstairs in front of the TV.

"You can shower here. I'll join you," Gord shouted after Eve who was already halfway down the stairs. "Gah," Gord said to himself trying to decide if he should get up and chase after Eve or go back to sleep.

"I'll call you later," Eve yelled up the stairs. Sleep it is. And just like that, Eve was out the door and on her way to her place. She dialed Will with her Bluetooth on the way. Will gave her the good news that April was eligible for bail and due to the circumstances of her crime, no bail bond was required at this time.

"I'm heading to the station to complete the paperwork. April should be out later today."

"I'll see you there," Eve said, sounding relieved to have her assistant back. Eve would have to get over herself. April was irreplaceable.

* * *

Cynthia couldn't help but bound into the kitchen behind Gayle, excited she may have a way to free April and still meet David's demands.

"Mom! I have an idea!" Cynthia was too excited to wait for Gayle to turn her attention from the coffee pot before she continued. "I think we can get April out of jail and it's so easy I don't know why I didn't think of it before."

"What? Really?"

"We just need to come up with some bail money. Do you and Dad have any savings?"

"Well . . ."

"I don't think we have to have the cash right now. I was researching how bail works online last night and . . ."

"Cynthia, it's okay. Whatever it takes to get your dad back. We need to do it. Yes, we have some investments we can cash in. Do you know how much we need?"

"No. It's usually determined by the judge based on the crime and how big a flight risk he thinks April is. I'll go down to the station and see if they will give me any of that information. Is that okay? Do you mind watching Luke?"

"Of course not. Go."

"We're going to get him back, Mom," Cynthia said as she hugged Gayle more tightly than she had in years. Gayle started to tear up. "Tell Luke I love him, and I'll be back soon." Cynthia grabbed her bag which contained the file she got from Linda. She remembered what Ben told her about the PPC audit and that she needed to call the shareholders and find out what that mysterious $10,000 was about. "Hey, how did it go having Ben here last night?"

"He and Luke seemed to have a lot of fun. I felt a little bad going to bed when Luke did and leaving Ben by himself, but I was just so tired after everything."

"I'm sure he understood. I'll call you as soon as I find out anything," Cynthia said heading out the door.

On the way to the police station, Cynthia dialed the number of the shareholders she needed to talk to.

"Hello," came a woman's voice from Cynthia's Bluetooth speakers.

"Hi. Is this Mrs. Wright?"

"Yes, it is."

"Hi, Mrs. Wright. This is Cynthia Webber from Darlington & Associates." Cynthia winced as she said where she was calling from. She hated lying to the woman, but she felt it was the only way she would see her. She'd hoped Mrs. Wright would have no way of knowing she was just fired.

"Hi, Cynthia. Are you the auditor for PPC?"

"Yes," Cynthia winced again. "Well, actually I'm only part of the audit team. I'm sorry to call you on the weekend, but I have a quick question for you regarding a transaction that was recorded in your PPC shareholder loan account."

"Wouldn't that be better answered by our bookkeeper?" Mrs. Wright probed, sounding a little confused.

"It would be easier if I could explain in person. Do you have time for a quick meeting today? I'm happy to meet you wherever is convenient."

"Can you be here in an hour?" Cynthia was surprised that Mrs. Wright was available so quickly and while she wasn't sure how long she would be at the police station, she didn't want to miss her opportunity.

"Yes. Where would you like to meet?"

"Are you familiar with the Mackenzie Square area of town?"

"Of course."

"We're number 121 on the Close."

"Alright. I will see you in an hour. Thank you so much for agreeing to meet me on such short notice." Cynthia felt a little flushed as she realized Mackenzie Square was almost as far south as you could get which meant she would only have about thirty minutes at the police station. That would have to do.

"Of course. What did you say your name was again, dear?"

"Cynthia."

"Right. Cynthia. Well, we definitely want to make sure our investment in PPC is being taken care of. Whatever you need, Cynthia."

"Thank you, Mrs. Wright. I'll see you soon." Almost as soon as Cynthia was off the line with Mrs. Wright, there was ringing on her car stereo. She clicked the phone line on from her steering wheel and started to talk when the voice on the other end cut her off.

"Cyn? You there?"

"I'm here, Linda. Geez, you didn't give me half a chance to answer, girl."

"She's in! She's fucking in!!"

"Whoa, language. It's too early for that shit," Cynthia laughed at her friend.

"Oh my god, I'm sorry. Is Luke in the car?"

"No, it's fine. What's going on? Who's in?"

"Kat Wilde. She's willing to talk about David and how he bribed her. I just got off the phone with her. It took a little convincing, but once she heard your story, she wanted to help. She's flying in as soon as she can. Maybe even later today."

"That's amazing! I'm working on something that might help too," Cynthia said, thinking about her meeting with Mrs. Wright. "I'm just headed to the police station to see about bailing April out. Can you meet me there or do you have a hot story you've got to cover?"

"Actually, you bailing April out might be a pretty hot story. I'm sorry, I know you don't like being in the spotlight, but you're in the middle of my biggest story. We really should do a proper interview."

"Shit. I was wondering when it would come to this," Cynthia said with a sigh, her eyes still fixed on the road. "I'll think about it. Are you coming to the station?"

"Already on my way," Linda said, grabbing her coat from the hook on her office door.

48

He wasn't sure what time it was, but Bob knew the sun had been up for a couple of hours, so it must have been about seven or eight in the morning. He watched the pink prairie sunrise while figuring out how he was going to get out of the trailer before David came back. After finding a loaded gun in the top drawer of the trailer's kitchen, Bob managed to cut himself on the knife that was also in the drawer. He didn't mind though. The cut wasn't very deep, and the knife served him well as he managed to cut his ankles free from the zip strip.

Having full use of his legs again and a gun for protection, Bob curled up in the bed at the back of the trailer. It smelled so bad; he wondered when the last time the sheets had been washed and decided to lay on top of the bed, making a blanket out of a coat he found in the closet. Remembering old stories his buddies had told him about working in the oil patch, he could only imagine what that bed had been used for. Luckily, he was tired and sore enough he quickly fell asleep with the gun by his side.

The sunrise found Bob feeling pretty good considering his condition, but he couldn't lift his right arm higher than his waist without causing excruciating pain. From the looks of the bandage David prepared, the bleeding had slowed or maybe even stopped. Bob stared out the trailer window at the construction site that lay in front of him wondering if any of the equipment might have the keys in it. He thought about driving them off-site and finding help by drawing attention to himself that way, but the equipment seemed so far away. Although he was feeling better than yesterday, he wanted to conserve as much energy as possible.

Bob was pondering his options when he looked up to see the Escalade heading in the direction of the trailer. Shit. Whatever he was going to do, he'd have to act fast. He looked down at the gun by his side. As much as he would like to kill David, he wasn't a murderer. He'd barely shot a gun before but using it now would be his only hope. Between the Escalade and the trailer sat a welding truck. Bob had no idea what the repercussions of his actions might be. What he did know was there might be a chance he'd be sacrificing himself to take David out. He felt it was the only way.

His injured arm was mostly useless, and Bob was nervous about how accurate his shot would be with his non-dominant hand. He slid the back window of the trailer open as he watched the Escalade get closer. Wincing in pain as he lifted his arm to the window, he realised his suspicions. He was going to have to use his left hand to do most of the work. He rested his arm on the open window sill, took a deep breath, and steadied himself as he aimed the gun at the gas cylinder on the back of the welding truck. And then he pulled the trigger.

49

April stared at the graffiti on her cell wall, wondering what other prisoners could have possibly used to scratch the paint on the concrete bricks. She heard the sliding door where she once entered to visit Eve and looked up to see Eve escorted by Will Bronsky and the on-duty officer assigned to monitor the prison cells.

"What's going on?" April asked, surprised to see everyone.

"You made bail." Will sat down as the officer stepped outside of the visiting area.

"Is there any news about Kurt? Have they found his killer yet?"

"Not yet." Eve looked at Will as she started to update April on Kurt's murder. "They're calling it a revenge killing. The police think it was either someone from PPC or someone who would have a lot to lose if the pipeline were shut down. They could have left the body at the construction site to implicate PPC."

"When can I get out of here? I need to find out what happened." Tears filled April's eyes. The night alone in the cell had made her more emotional than usual. The door opened behind Eve and Will. There stood the officer with Cynthia by his side.

"You've got another visitor," the officer said. "It's getting a little crowded in here, don't you think?" Will stood up and offered his chair to Cynthia.

"It's alright. I've got some paperwork to attend to so April can be on her way." Will nodded to Cynthia as they passed each other in the small visiting area.

"I know you don't know me." Cynthia started shaking as she sat down. "I used to work for David Jerew. Do you know who that is?" Cynthia asked April.

"Unfortunately, I do. I'm sorry you had the displeasure of working for that bastard. He didn't send you, did he?" April's eyes squinted slightly as she looked with resentment at Cynthia.

"Well, in a roundabout way, I guess he did. He's holding my dad hostage until I get you out of jail." Cynthia tried to muster a solemn smile. Eve and April both breathed in a sharp breath of shock.

"He just doesn't know when to quit." April was clearly agitated. "I'm so sorry he's done this to your family. I've had a restraining order against him for years. I knew he was following me, but I didn't bother reporting him. He's a deadbeat dad, but I never thought he would do anything like this."

"I'm not sure what this means for my dad now that you're going to be out on bail and I wasn't responsible for that. You should know that I reported David to the police when he took my dad. He's a wanted man."

"I hope you find your dad, but I can't help you. I need to find out what happened to my boyfriend. He was gunned down at the PPC construction site." April paused to look at the floor in contemplation. "I wish it had been David instead. We would both be a lot happier right now."

"I understand," Cynthia said trying to hide her disappointment. Sirens blazed outside the station, and there was a commotion in the hallway. The officer outside the cell had disappeared. "Would you call me if you think of anything that might help find my dad?"

"Sure. Do you know Dr. Greenwich from the university?"

"I'm so sorry," Cynthia said turning to face Dr. Greenwich. "I was so focused on talking to April that I didn't really notice you sitting there." Eve and Cynthia exchanged numbers and agreed to call the other if they heard anything from David.

"Cynthia! Get out here!" Linda called running down the hall. "There's been an explosion at the PPC pipeline."

"What?!" Cynthia was out the door in a flash without saying a word to Eve or April who sat looking at each other, confusion in their eyes.

50

"**Wait! Oh my god**. I can't go with you." Cynthia's eyes were welling up with tears as she stopped in front of Linda's vehicle outside the police station. She was sure her dad was at the construction site. "There's something I need to do. It might help bring David down. I'm not sure yet, but I need to find out, and I have to be there in thirty minutes. There's no way I'll get there in time if I go to the PPC site." Cynthia took a deep breath and wiped tears from her cheeks. "Keep me posted, okay?" she asked walking backwards towards her car. "I'll get there as soon as I can."

"You got it. Are you okay to go alone?" Linda asked.

"I think it's the only way I can do this." Cynthia managed a closed-lipped, half smile for her friend. Linda blew her a kiss and was on her way to meet the news van at the construction site. Cynthia decided to go straight to Mrs. Wright's. At least it was Saturday, and she didn't have to deal with rush hour traffic. She might even be a few minutes early.

Cynthia arrived at 121 Mackenzie Close right on time. The Wright's house wasn't as impressive as Cynthia imagined for two people owning majority shares in the largest pipeline company in the country. Cynthia still couldn't believe PPC hadn't gone public by now. She took a deep breath in and exhaled as she pressed her finger to the ivory coloured doorbell. The door opened immediately, and a well-put-together woman in her late forties greeted Cynthia warmly.

"Come on in, dear."

"Thank you, Mrs. Wright."

"You can call me Helen. Mrs. Wright makes me feel old, but I appreciate you extending me the courtesy of formalities. You don't see that much in young people these days." Helen smiled at Cynthia as she closed the door behind her. "We can talk in here." Helen motioned to a room behind her and to the left. Cynthia slipped off her shoes and followed Helen into her home office. "How was the traffic this morning?"

"Not bad, actually." Cynthia tried not to let her mind wander to the explosion and her dad. She had an important job to do. "Helen, I'm sure you're a busy lady. Do you mind if I get straight to the point this morning?"

"Not at all, dear. I wish you would, actually. I have nothing to hide, and I'm happy to give you whatever information you need. The financial statements are due to be presented at a board meeting early next week. I'm surprised they aren't finished yet."

"Actually, they are finished, but something didn't seem right to me. Every year, we get all the shareholders to sign off on the transactions going through their accounts. All the money they've taken out of the company, and all the personal money they've deposited into the company bank account."

"But we don't take any money out of PPC. It's too much of a hassle, and we have other companies we can withdraw funds from." Helen seemed confused. "But I don't remember seeing the transactions this year. I remember signing off on them last year though."

"I brought the transaction list with me. Here you go," Cynthia said, handing over the general ledger print out of the Wright's shareholder loan account.

"This $10,000 withdrawal isn't right. Are you sure this is our account? We don't take large lump sums like that out of PPC. It must be some kind of bookkeeping error." Helen rolled her eyes and made a sound under her breath that Cynthia couldn't make out.

"I'll look into it and let you know," Cynthia said, taking the paper back from Helen. "That was the only question I had for you. If you'll excuse me, I need to check on the explosion at the PPC construction site." Without realizing what she just said, Cynthia stood up and turned towards the office door. It looked as though Helen was processing what she just heard.

"What did you say? Explosion?"

"Yes, it happened right before I left to come here. It's probably on the news by now." Cynthia thought of Linda reporting on the explosion, flames in the background, as her dad burned in the mess. She took a slow breath and shook her head. No, you don't know that, Cynthia. It didn't take long for Helen to find the story on TV. There was Linda, just as Cynthia predicted. She was standing in front of a vehicle that had been turned on its side. It looked like . . . No, could it be? It was a black Escalade. This realization snapped Cynthia out of the trance-like state she'd fallen into watching her friend report on the fire. Emergency crews were working in the background.

Cynthia realized she needed to get on the road, but she wasn't exactly sure where she was headed.

"Thank you so much for your help, Helen. I'll be in touch as soon as I find out what's going on with that entry."

"Thank you, dear," Helen said as she escorted Cynthia to the door.

51

Once in her car, Cynthia dialed Ben, fearing she might forget about the PPC bookkeeping once she started dealing with the physical chaos that was her life right now. She got his voicemail as she figured she might. Saturdays during audit season were just like any other day of the week. Even though it was just a recording, the sound of his voice made her feel better somehow—like everything was going to work out.

"Hi, Ben. It's Cynthia. I just met with Helen Wright. Any chance that the $10,000 is a bookkeeping error? I'm guessing you probably already checked that, but Helen says they don't withdraw that kind of money from PPC. I'm heading out to the construction site right now. Not sure if you've heard, but there was an explosion out there about an hour ago. Call me later. Thanks." Cynthia started her car to head out on the road. She wanted to go to the construction site, but she wasn't sure she would be able to get any information with emergency and news crews doing their jobs. She thought it best to check on her mom and Luke instead. Gayle would be hysterical if she'd turned on the news and saw what was going on, and Cynthia needed a hug from Luke more than ever.

Cynthia switched on the radio to distract her from all that was going on. The audit trail in PPC's books was in Ben's hands. There was nothing she could do now that she wasn't a D&A employee. Cynthia felt her energy would be best spent keeping her mom and Luke calm and occupied until her dad was found.

The ringing on her Bluetooth interrupted her thoughts.

"Hello," she said as she pressed the answer button on her steering wheel.

"Cyn, it's me. I've got good news and bad news." Linda's voice echoed in stereo.

"Better give me the bad news first."

"Your dad is missing. There's evidence he was here, but nobody can tell what happened to him which is also the good news. It looks like he wasn't near the explosion. The police still need to do a full investigation, but from what the fire chief told me, they're almost positive it's only equipment in that fire."

"I saw a vehicle behind you on the TV news report. What's the story there?"

"Looks like it was knocked on its side from the blast. The driver was taken to the hospital. It wasn't David. They think he asked someone to check on your dad for him. Cyn, we need to go live with this whole story; it's just getting too complicated. I need to interview you. Maybe it will bring David out of hiding, and we can find your dad faster?"

"Yeah, I've been thinking about that too. You're right," Cynthia sighed. The last thing she wanted to do was be on TV, but if it helped find her dad, then she needed to do it. "I'm headed to my mom's. Give me some time to fill her in on what's happened. Can you meet me there in an hour? We can figure out our next move."

"You got it. We're going to find your dad, Cyn. I can feel it, and you know how good my instincts are."

"Yes, that's what makes you so good at your job. You always know where the good stories are. See you soon." Cynthia hung up and noticed she had a message waiting. She was almost at her parents' and decided she would check it when she got there. Hopefully, it wasn't more bad news.

52

As Cynthia pulled in to the driveway, she noticed her mom and Luke making a snowman in the backyard. Cynthia dialed her voicemail to check her message before joining them. It was Ben.

"Cynthia, I've checked the bookkeeping. It wasn't an error, and I've discovered something else. This is bigger than I thought. I think we need to get Sam involved, but I want to talk to you first. Can you meet me after work? Text me the time and place, and I'll be there." Cynthia wasn't sure what to think of Ben's cryptic message, but she knew she needed to meet him. She texted him the time and place and prayed that nothing would come up to prevent her from going to the meeting. By this time, Luke had noticed Cynthia sitting in the driveway and was starting to make his way over to the car. Cynthia closed her eyes for a split second, trying to prepare to break the news to Gayle about the explosion and the interview Linda wanted to do. She grabbed her bag and hopped out of the car.

"Hey, buddy! I missed you. I sure like your snowman." Cynthia knelt and gave Luke a big bear hug. "Hi, Mom," Cynthia said with a wave as Gayle came over.

"How did it go at the police station?" Gayle was anxious for any news about Bob.

"Well, April is out on bail, but nobody seems to know where David is. He has just disappeared. Linda wants to do a news story to lure him out. She's coming over in about an hour to discuss it."

"Whatever she thinks will help is fine with me. I'm sure if this had happened to any other family, she would have done the story already."

"Yes, I think you're right, Mom. There's something else." Cynthia glanced at Luke as she said it, signalling to Gayle that it was an adult conversation. She turned her attention to Luke. "Why don't you head inside and we'll all have some hot chocolate together. Auntie Linda is coming over in a little while." Cynthia opened the door for Luke, and he wandered in without protest. From the looks of his snowsuit, he and Gayle had been playing outside for a while. Cynthia hoped this meant Gayle hadn't seen the news about the explosion. She closed the door behind Luke and turned to Gayle. There was no time for Cynthia to gently break the news to Gayle.

"Mom, there was an explosion at the PPC construction site. The police thought Dad might have been held there, but he's still missing." Cynthia put her arm around Gayle. "Linda thinks sharing our story and what David has done to our family, will help. We need to stay positive right now." Gayle nodded. She looked as though she was about to burst into tears, but Cynthia knew her mom was strong, and she'd be able to hold it together for Luke. "All we can do now is wait for Linda and plan our next move."

* * *

There was no way April was leaving the police station without answers. As hard as Eve tried to convince April to let the officers do their jobs, April was determined to get information.

"Look, Miss Sundin, you just made bail. I realize the crime you could potentially be charged with happened by accident, but I still recommend you stay out of trouble until your trial is over." Detective Bain urged April to drop her line of questioning.

"I'm not a criminal. I never meant for anyone to get hurt. I threw my shoe at him when other protestors were throwing rocks for crying out loud. There's something you should know. I don't know if it will help you find my dad; I know he's a wanted man right now. David Jerew."

"David Jerew's your father?"

"I'm afraid so. He's been stalking me for months which is a violation of the restraining order I have against him. I didn't mention it earlier because he only ever just sat in his vehicle and watched me while I was at school. But he's a dangerous man. I'm surprised it didn't come to the surface sooner. He threatened my mother's life several times when I was living with her. Check the restraining order paperwork."

"Thank you, Miss Sundin. I will look into it. It appears your father has a past that has caught up with him. Why don't you go home and get some rest? I can't give information to anyone other than Kurt's next of kin, and so far, we've been unable to locate anyone."

"That's because Kurt didn't have any next of kin," Eve spoke up from behind April. "If there's anything we can do to help, Detective, please let us know."

"Thank you, Dr. Greenwich. I appreciate that."

53

Bob was thankful to be on his way to get the medical attention he needed. After he fired at the welding truck, he left the trailer and took off towards the highway. He tucked the handgun in his pants and covered it up with his shirt, so it didn't draw any unwanted attention to him. It was bad enough that it was clear he had been shot and had been bleeding. He didn't know who had been driving the Escalade and he didn't care. All that mattered to him was getting to the hospital. He felt safe knowing he had a gun and could use it if he had to. You just never knew who might pick up a hitchhiker these days.

Once on the back road leading to the highway, Bob started to slow down. He realized he probably should have waited at the construction site for emergency vehicles to arrive, but he couldn't take a chance on whoever was driving the Escalade seeing him and preventing him from getting the help he needed. A couple of vehicles had already happened along the service road, but the drivers were both women. He didn't blame them for not stopping. He always told Cynthia never to stop for hitchhikers. It just wasn't safe.

Before long, an old pickup truck slowed next to Bob.

"Looks like you could use some help," the driver said, leaning towards the passenger window, he'd rolled down.

"Sure could," Bob replied. "Do you think you could drop me off at the hospital?" The driver stopped the truck and got out to help Bob into the passenger side. "Thank you. You have no idea how much this means to me."

"I think I do. You look pretty rough. I'm Earl."

"Thanks, Earl. I'm Bob."

"Let's get you to the hospital."

* * *

Cynthia realized she hadn't eaten breakfast and it was almost 11:00 a.m. already. She put some water on to boil for tea and hot chocolate and opened the fridge door. Lasagna. It was always a good time for her mom's lasagna, and she was thankful there was still some leftovers.

"Anybody else want some lasagna with their hot chocolate?"

"Can I have some cookies, Mommy?" Normally, Cynthia would make Luke wait until after lunch, but given the craziness of the last couple of days, she was just happy Luke was eating.

"Sure, baby, that probably goes a lot better with hot chocolate than lasagna. I'm just so hungry." Cynthia made a face as she exaggerated the word hungry and Luke laughed. Their moment was interrupted by the phone. "Do you want me to get that, Mom?"

"Sure, honey, go ahead." Cynthia put her lasagna on the counter and picked up the phone. "Roberts residence," Cynthia said, sounding official. There was a pause while Cynthia listened to the person on the other end of the line.

"Really? Thank you so much. We'll be there as soon as we can." Tears of joy ran down Cynthia's cheeks as she hung up the phone. She looked at Gayle as she ran to hug Luke. "Grandpa is in the hospital. It looks like he's going to be just fine."

"We have to get to the hospital, grab your coat." Gayle clasped her heart as she headed towards the door.

"Mom, I can't. Linda will be here any minute. Tell Dad I'll be there as soon as I can. Linda and I need to get David out of hiding so the police can do their job and arrest him."

As if summoned by the mention of her name, Linda appeared at the back door. Cynthia opened the door for her friend then walked to the microwave to grab her lasagna.

"Lasagna?" she held up a plate towards Linda.

"Yes! I'm starving," Linda replied. "How are you holding up Gayle?"

"Better than I was five minutes ago. The hospital called and Bob's there now. They said he's going to be okay. Luke and I are heading over there."

"That's amazing," Linda said, hugging Gayle. "I'm so glad they found him. Okay, Cyn, here's what's going to happen," Linda said, turning to Cynthia. "I thought it might be best if we focus on the facts leading up to today. I'll start outside and introduce the story a little then you and I can chat in the kitchen if that's okay with you?" Linda looked at Cynthia for agreement.

"Of course, whatever you need."

"You ready?"

"You know me. I just want to get this over with, so I can go see my dad." Cynthia and Linda finished their lasagna as they talked more about the interview.

"Alright, this isn't going to be a live interview, so we can stop anytime you need a break. I'm going to head outside and talk to my crew. Then we'll come back inside and interview you. It will probably take less than 30 minutes unless we need to do retakes."

"When will the interview air?" Cynthia asked.

"I can probably get it on the 5 o'clock news," Linda replied. "It'll be dark by then. Maybe David will come out of hiding looking for April. I should give Detective Bain a heads-up in case he wants to put officers on April. She might be in danger." Linda checked for food in her teeth with a mirror from her purse then was off to talk with her crew.

54

"**I need to speak** with the police," was the first thing Bob said when he got out of surgery.

"It's nice to see you awake, Mr. Roberts. How are you feeling?" Bob's nurse was busily straightening his pillows and making sure he was warm enough. "The police are waiting to talk with you about the gun you had in your possession. Do you remember the gun?"

"Yes, of course. I gave it to you and asked you to call the police before I went into surgery." Bob sounded a little agitated that his nurse implied he wouldn't remember.

As if reading his mind, Bob's nurse looked at him and said, "I'm sorry, the anesthetic sometimes makes people's memories a little fuzzy. I'll go get the detective for you."

"Thank you." Bob smiled in apology for his agitation. Detective Bain entered his room almost as soon as the nurse left.

"Good afternoon, Mr. Roberts. I understand you were taken hostage by David Jerew. He took you from your home?"

"Yes, he took me to the PPC construction site and left me for dead. Or, so I thought anyway. Last night he tossed a bag with a burger and fries in it into the trailer where he left me."

"So, you were in the foreman's trailer?"

"Yes, I think so. Have you found that bastard?"

"No, I'm afraid Mr. Jerew is still missing. He paid someone to drive his vehicle and leave that food for you. It appears Mr. Jerew is good at hiding. Is there anything you remember he said or did that might help us find him?" Detective Bain looked hopeful for some useful information.

"He talked a lot about his daughter, April, and how it was because of my daughter that he couldn't see her. Something about Cynthia being responsible for his daughter's arrest."

"Well, his daughter turned herself in, and she's out on bail now, so we are keeping a close watch over her in case Mr. Jerew tries to contact her. We are also issuing a plea to the public to try and help us locate Mr. Jerew. Your daughter will be on the news later with her reporter friend. We think once the public hears Cynthia's story, anyone with information about Mr. Jerew will come forward. We also have an ex-cop helping us out. She caught David once before, and we think she may have some information that will help us. Thanks to that reporter Ms. Reeves. Were you responsible for the explosion at the construction site?"

"Yes, I saw a black Escalade coming down the road, and I thought it was David. I aimed at a cylinder on the back of a welding truck, hoping what you see in the movies is true, you know?" Detective Bain nodded. "Once the explosion went off and knocked the Escalade on its side, I got the hell out of there as fast as I could."

"And where did the gun come from?"

"I found it in the trailer." Bob shivered remembering his shock when he touched the cold metal barrel in the drawer of the trailer. "I guess I'm lucky it was loaded. You have it now, right?"

"Yes. The lab has it and is running tests on it as we speak. Is there anything else you remember that could help us locate Mr. Jerew?"

"I don't think so. Can I see my family now?"

"Of course. Call me if you remember anything else," Detective Bain said, placing his business card on the bedside table. Bob nodded and shook the detective's hand.

55

Gayle, Cynthia, and Luke returned from the hospital, feeling relieved but tired. Cynthia was able to meet her mom and Luke there after her interview with Linda. Bob was required to stay overnight for observation and to make sure there weren't any complications as a result of his shoulder surgery. Luke and Gayle went into the living room to play with Luke's toys. Cynthia needed to get ready to meet Ben and find out what he had uncovered in the PPC files, but she returned a message from Linda first.

"Hey, Cyn."

"Hey. Can you talk now?" Cynthia knew the ex-cop Katrina Wilde was in town and Linda had already met with her. Cynthia was anxious to find out what Katrina's history with David was.

"Yep, I'm good to go, and I have good news. Katrina, or Kat, as she prefers to be called, is willing to tell the police the whole story from when she was on the force and working undercover as a prostitute. David tried to hire her for sex, and when she busted him, he bribed her to let him go and leave town. At first, she wouldn't take his money and continued with the arrest, but then he beat the crap out of her and threatened to hurt her family if she talked. Kat was afraid and humiliated David beat her. She thought she would get fired for taking the money, so she left town without saying a word to Detective Bain."

"Jesus Christ! That asshole's been threatening women for a long time. I wonder who else he's threatened or hurt? How long ago did you say this was?

"Seven years. Kat's been in Denver ever since. She started a PI business to help women gather the evidence they need to put asshat's like David away. She apologized for not wanting to get involved with your case when I talked to her earlier. She was embarrassed she left Calgary so fast. Once I gave her all the details of what David's been doing, she wanted to help us find him and put him away for good. She's going to talk to her old boss, Detective Bain, and come clean about what really happened."

"That's great!" Cynthia checked the time as she said it. "I better get going. I've got to meet Ben pretty quick."

"What's happening with the hunky Mr. Ben?"

"Oh please, you're terrible." Cynthia felt her cheeks flush. "Didn't I tell you? He found something else in the books of PPC. Actually, it sounded like he found a lot of things. Our senior manager is willing to get involved as well. Or, I guess he's my ex-senior manager. Anyway, it's strictly business."

"Oh, that's too bad. You could use a little fun, my friend."

"I'll call you later," Cynthia said, ignoring Linda's implications.

"Be careful. Your interview will be airing soon. Who knows what that will bring out in David."

"I will."

Cynthia arrived at Ben's at the time she had texted him earlier—5:00 p.m. on the dot. She knew Ben would probably be going back to work after their meeting. Ben buzzed her into the building and told her to come right up as the door was unlocked. Cynthia entered Ben's apartment and took her coat and boots off at the door. She couldn't see the TV from the door, but she could hear her interview was on.

Just five days ago, Cynthia Webber found the body of Jim Dunn, Controller of Prairie Pipeline Company, stuffed inside the very pipe that's caused so much controversy for his company. What followed Ms. Webber's discovery was a series of bizarre events leading to her wrongful dismissal from Darlington & Associates, one of the city's largest accounting firms. Since being fired, Ms. Webber has been harassed and stalked by her ex-boss, David Jerew, culminating in a hostage situation at the home of Ms. Webber's parents where Mr. Jerew shot Bob Roberts and took him hostage. Thankfully, Mr. Roberts is now resting safely at the hospital, but Mr. Jerew's whereabouts are unknown. Earlier today I interviewed Ms. Webber. Here's what she had to say . . .

As Cynthia walked into Ben's living room, she saw Sam sitting across from Ben. She paused for a moment, not sure what to expect.

"There she is. The star of the hour," Sam said, nodding to Cynthia. Ben turned down the volume on the TV.

"I'm glad they found your dad." Ben stood up as Cynthia entered the room. "Can I get you something to drink?"

"No, thank you, I brought my water," Cynthia said, holding up her water bottle.

"I hope you don't mind Sam joining us. He has some information to share as well."

"Of course not. I thought he might be here." Cynthia sat down on the couch next to Ben. Ben's laptop was open to the PPC file.

"I checked for any bookkeeping errors, and unfortunately it's not that." Ben had a disappointed look on his face as he continued. "The $10,000 withdrawal from the Wright's shareholder loan account came directly out of the bank account as a cash withdrawal. There's no record whatsoever of what that cash was used for."

"Who has signing authority to withdraw that much cash without any kind of approval process?" Cynthia looked from Ben to Sam, hoping there was a logical explanation to the mess they'd stumbled upon.

"That's another problem," Sam answered. "Gord James, the CFO, has signing authority on the account, and while that in itself is not unusual, I checked the banking documentation provided for the audit. It's normally Gord and a board member that sign paycheques, but Gord has the ability sign without a board member if a board member is unavailable during payroll processing times. It's been like this for years, but nobody has ever questioned it."

"But that's a major violation of internal control," Cynthia was almost angry at her ex-senior manager who should know better. "Why wasn't this noticed in the past? I thought it was weird PPC still doesn't use direct deposit, but that's beside the point."

"Well, Cynthia, I think it's my fault it was never brought up in past audits, and that's the main reason I'm here now. I want to make this right. It's been too many years of David signing off on financial statements that don't meet proper auditing standards, and I've just stood by feeling powerless to do anything about it. When Ben came to me today questioning the Wright's shareholder loan account, I was almost relieved that someone else saw the error." Sam looked at the floor, embarrassed that he hadn't said anything sooner. "In the four years I've worked on the PPC audit, there have been similar transactions to what's happened in the Wright's account this year. The amount is usually right around the $10,000 mark, but in several smaller payments, so it doesn't look suspicious. A thousand here and a thousand there over the course of a year and nobody really questions it, but it still adds up to about $10,000, and it's always cash that's been withdrawn from the bank account with no record of what it's being used for. It's always in a different shareholder loan account. It seems like this year, whoever took the cash got sloppy."

"But didn't the shareholders sign off on their account transactions in the past?" Cynthia was in awe of what Sam was telling her. "And who codes the bookkeeping transactions?"

"The original documentation for the withdrawal slips just say, 'shareholder draw', and that's if you can find a slip. For some transactions, there's nothing at all. And the shareholders didn't always sign off on their account, just like the Wright's didn't sign off on theirs this year. It's always noted as non-material in the file and left at that. It seems like the cash is strategically being taken out of different shareholder accounts each year."

"Looks like we've opened a real can of worms." Cynthia looked at Sam. "So, you've seen this pattern all along?"

"Yes, but I didn't think anything of it until this year. There are some shareholders who don't pay that close attention to their accounts, and they sign off because they trust David. Now that I've seen what David is capable of, I'm going to file a report with the CPA ethics board, and I plan to write a report for PPC's audit committee as well. They are likely going to want to find a replacement for Gord and probably new auditors too." Cynthia nodded in agreement as Ben raised his eyebrows.

"And D&A will likely be one partner short if David ever comes out from hiding."

56

Gord James flicked off the TV. His face was expressionless as he sat in the dark, scotch in hand. He feared David the minute he met him five years ago, but he knew David would get the job done and that's precisely why he'd hired him as PPC's auditor. What he didn't realize was what David was capable of. He thought about Cynthia and her family and wondered what else David might do and to whom. Gord was the kind of man that didn't bother with locking his door, but tonight he felt the urge.

The PPC audit went well the first year David handled it, but then he got greedy. He told Gord he wanted a cash supplement to maintain a clean audit report free of objections. Of course, Gord wasn't going to use his own money, so he stole it from the company. He felt the shareholders owed him anyway for all the nights he'd stayed late and the weekends he'd worked when he could have been playing squash. Two years ago, Gord had enough, and he told David he wasn't going to pay anymore, and he was going to report David to the CPA ethics board. David rebutted and threatened Gord, holding it over his head that he'd gone along with David's plan. Gord knew he would be fired from PPC and would never find work in the city again, so he continued to steal from the shareholders and pay David the cash he wanted. He was just thankful David hadn't raised his price over the years—although he'd threatened that too.

Gord felt the pounding of his heart in his throat as a sudden surge of anxiety and fear came over him. He put his hands over his face and closed his eyes as he realized what it meant for him if the police found David. The way he saw it, he had two choices: leave town and start a new life and a new career somewhere else or tell the cops what he'd been doing all these years and hope they'd go easy on him. He'd still have to find a new career. David was right. Nobody in this country, let alone this city, would hire him as an accountant after he'd been stealing from the very people he worked for. He would most certainly lose his CPA designation. Gord shot back the rest of his scotch, returned his head to his hands and cried like a baby.

* * *

"Are you serious?" Linda couldn't believe what Troy was telling her.

"Why would I make that up? The guys in ballistics confirmed that the bullet found in Kurt Ripple's skull was fired from the gun that Bob Roberts found in the trailer at the PPC construction site." Troy was exhausted, and all he wanted to do was enjoy a nice dinner with Linda, but he knew she was going to grill him about work the whole time. He scooped up a mouthful of Caesar salad looking forward to chewing rather than talking.

"I guess that makes sense since his body was found there. Maybe the killer planned on coming back for the gun. Or maybe the killer works at PPC?"

"Or maybe the killer just wanted everyone to think he or she works at PPC. That would be the most obvious alternative. Environmental protester goes a little overboard, disgruntled pipeline employee who has had enough decides to shut him up. Or maybe it was a friend of Jim's seeking revenge. Shall we just let the good detective do his job?"

"You're right. I've got to talk to Detective Bain." Linda had a spark in her eyes Troy had seen many times before. She loved her job; there was no doubting that.

"Well, do you think you could talk to him *after* we have dinner?"

"Of course, I'm sorry. I just want to see this case solved."

"So you can move on to your next story, I know. Do you think we could put work on the backburner for now?" Linda smiled a sheepish smile and slowly nodded in reply.

"You know, I think I might have a glass of wine."

* * *

Gord took a deep breath. He knew what he needed to do. He was tired of feeling like a coward. He dialed the number he'd seen on the TV after Linda's interview with Cynthia.

"Hello, this is Gord James. I have some information Detective Bain may be interested in. Is he available?"

"I'm sorry, the detective is out of the office, would you like to make an appointment?"

"Yes, please. I'll take the first thing he's got." Gord was tempted to hang up and back out, but he thought about Eve and how he had her arrested based on false assumptions. At least this was something he could try and make right.

"Alright, the detective will see you in twelve hours, Mr. James, tomorrow 7:00 a.m."

"Thank you."

57

Cynthia was still reeling from her meeting with Ben and Sam. She couldn't believe the PPC shareholders had been stolen from for at least four years without anyone doing anything about it. When she left Ben's, Ben and Sam were getting ready to head back to the office and were planning the reports they needed to write for both the PPC audit committee and the CPA ethics board. As Cynthia pulled in to Gayle and Bob's driveway, she felt sick about what David had gotten away with all these years. It made her eyes sting with anger. How could a person who's supposed to be a trusted advisor do something so terrible?

As Cynthia got out of her car, she glanced up towards the backyard. She saw a tiny glowing orange light she hadn't noticed before. Then she saw a reflection off the glasses behind the light as she realized it was the cherry of a cigarette David was puffing on. Cynthia wondered how David had gotten past the officers that had been trailing her. She froze, not sure what to do next. And then her anger kicked in. She felt an unbearable rage for all the ways David had tormented her and her family this week. Her face felt hot as she grabbed her bag from her car. How dare he show up here.

"You've got some nerve," Cynthia said as she walked up to David. "You know the police are looking for you, don't you?" David stood silently puffing on his smoke, enjoying every minute of Cynthia's outburst. A sly grin spread across his face.

"Soon they will be looking for you too, Ms. Webber."

"What are you talking about? I've done nothing wrong."

"Haven't you? Didn't you conspire with the CFO of PPC to steal money from the Wrights?"

"No, that was you!" Cynthia's blood boiled at the mention of the Wrights.

"Well, that's not what CPA has on record. I filed an ethics complaint against you two days ago that says you conspired with Gord James to steal money from PPC shareholders, and you were fired from D&A because of that."

"You know that's not true, and I have other employees who will back me up."

"You couldn't possibly. You don't even have access to D&A files anymore." Cynthia wasn't sure if David was bluffing about filing an ethics complaint against her, but she wasn't going to let him see her cards. She was confident Ben and Sam would file their complaint which would negate David's complaint against her. She had a major advantage over David—the truth. She also had friends that could back up her story. "And all that garbage in that interview you and Ms. Reeves did, nobody's going to believe that after they read what I have to say. You're merely a disgruntled employee striking out against your ex-employer who fired you for acting unethically." This hit Cynthia where it hurt. She knew how powerful the media was. Heck, it had worked to get David to come out of hiding.

David took a giant step towards Cynthia, so he was right in her face blowing his disgusting cigarette smoke at her. "You'll never work again once my side of the story comes out, Ms. Webber. I know you went to see the Wrights as an employee of D&A." David shoved Cynthia aside as he walked towards the road. Cynthia coughed and sputtered as the air cleared of tobacco. She knew what she had done was unethical, but she'd brushed it off for the greater good of finding answers.

"Wait!" Cynthia exclaimed, grasping for a way to keep David's untruths out of the media. "April wants to meet with you." Cynthia knew this was a lie, but it was the one thing she could think of that might keep David from releasing his little horror story about her. "Meet us in the university parking lot in an hour. You know, the one where you would spy on April from your Escalade." David stopped but didn't turn around. Cynthia wasn't sure if he was buying her lie.

"How do I know this isn't a trap and the minute I get there, you'll have the cops all over me? April has a restraining order against me."

"That never stopped you before." Cynthia tried to remain calm as she thought of how she could convince David to go to the university. "Come and check it out for yourself. Keep a low profile. If you see cops there, then leave, but if you want a chance to make things up to your daughter, it would be in your best interest to stay."

"We'll see," David said as he walked down the driveway and headed north along Bob and Gayle's street. Cynthia had no idea how he had arrived there. She followed him out to the road and watched as he walked a couple of blocks then turned right. He must have had a car waiting for him on the side street. Cynthia turned back towards the house. She saw her mom standing in the kitchen, looking out the window at her. She opened the back door as Cynthia got close.

"Are you okay? What are you doing out here?"

"David was here," Cynthia said, bracing for her mom's reaction.

"I'm calling the police," Gayle said in a hushed tone so Luke wouldn't hear.

"He's gone. It was just more threats, anyway. I guess David realized his attempts to hurt us didn't work, so he's gone back to trying to ruin my career now. It's a long story, but Ben and I discovered David's been stealing from his clients. Well, we're pretty sure it's David, anyway. I think he just confirmed that for me. He's filed a complaint with the CPA ethics committee making it look like I'm the one that's been stealing."

"But how can he do that?" Gayle was dumbfounded.

"I told a PPC client I worked for D&A after I had been fired so I could get a meeting with her to get information about their file." Cynthia felt tears welling up in her eyes. Could this be how David was going to end her career? Gayle put her arm around Cynthia, and Cynthia started to sob as the events from the past few days culminated.

"You need to call Detective Bain."

"I can't. There isn't time for that right now, but I have a plan. I just hope I can make it work. Do you trust me, Mom?"

"Of course, dear. I know you will have a long and prosperous accounting career. David won't get away with any of this." Cynthia wiped her eyes and blew her nose.

"I need to find Linda. I need her help. Can you watch Luke?"

"Yes, of course." Cynthia grabbed her purse and walked over to where Luke was playing in the living room.

"I'm so sorry to have to leave again, buddy. There's something really important I need to do. Adult stuff. I'll be back as soon as I can, okay? Grandma's going to play with you and read you lots of stories while I'm gone." Cynthia winked at Gayle. "I love you," Cynthia said as she gave Luke a big hug. She walked over to Gayle and hugged her too. "Thanks, Mom," she said as she grabbed her car keys off the table and headed out the door.

58

"It's been a really long time, Katrina." Detective Bain sat at his desk, still shocked that the woman sitting across from him was his former employee. She didn't even look like the same woman. Her blonde hair was now dark, and she looked tougher somehow, like you wouldn't want to run into her in a dark alley.

"Nobody calls me Katrina anymore. It's Kat."

"Alright, Kat. Well, I get the feeling this isn't a social call. Someone who takes off without so much as leaving a note doesn't show up after seven years just to say sorry." The detective was clearly angry about Kat's disappearance so many years ago. "You were a good cop. The force suffered when you left. We looked for you for months until we realized you didn't want to be found. The ultimate undercover gig."

"Well, I am sorry about that, Randy." Kat reached out and touched the detective's hand as she said it. He jerked his away.

"No. It doesn't work that way. You don't get to waltz in here and have everything forgiven just because you say sorry. I loved you, and you couldn't even tell me goodbye. You just left without so much as a note." Kat put her hand back in her lap.

"I'm sorry, Randy. I loved you too, but maybe it wasn't meant to be. All that sneaking around so our co-workers wouldn't find out was getting to be a bit much. But that's not the point. Something did happen to me, and that's why I'm here now. I need to tell you what happened." She looked at Detective Bain as if waiting for his approval to continue.

"Okay, I'm listening." Approval granted.

"Do you remember what I was doing when I left?"

"Of course. You were undercover in the sex crimes department. I worried about you every time you went out. I hated that you had that assignment. I thought the worst when you disappeared." Detective Bain stood up and started pacing the room. He couldn't look at Kat.

"Well, one night I guess I met my match. I tried to arrest a John, and he got really angry. Started shouting about me not knowing who he was and how he owned everyone in this town. He tried to pay me off. Told me to name my price and of course I wasn't having any of that. I told him I'd add bribing a cop to his list of offenses." Katrina paused and waited to see if Detective Bain was still listening. He hadn't stopped pacing since he stood up, but the silence made him take note. He stopped and looked at Kat, raising his eyebrows in acknowledgment. "That's when things got ugly. Turns out the guy had a gun tucked in his waistband. Before I knew what he was doing, he pulled it out and smacked me across the face with it." Detective Bain slammed his hand against the wall, stopped pacing and resumed his place at his desk across from Katrina.

"Did you know this bastard?"

"I didn't then, but I do now. When I left, I was scared. It wasn't the beating or the gun that scared me but the fact that this guy thought he could buy his way out of trouble. He struck me so hard it knocked me out. When I came to, I was cold and naked, and there was a pile of cash on my body and all around me. He raped me."

"Jesus, Katrina. Give me his name, and I'll have him arrested by the morning."

"It's not that easy. I didn't go to the hospital . . . or anywhere, for that matter. I took the money and left town. I just kept driving until I couldn't drive anymore. Eventually I ended up in Denver. I was too embarrassed to tell anyone until now. I didn't want anyone to know I had been raped and, in my mind,

I was a cop who took a bribe and let the perp get away."

"Fuck that! You were a damn good cop!"

"I'm sorry, Randy. I know I hurt you and I let you down." It was the thought of letting the man she loved down that caused the tears to roll down Kat's cheeks.

"So, why come back now?"

"You've got a damn good investigative reporter in this town. It turns out the man who did this to me so many years ago has started causing trouble again. I watched him for many years to make sure he wouldn't try and come after me or spread rumours about why I left. I think he assumed I took the money and ran. I did, but I've never forgotten David Jerew and what he did to me. Linda Reeves is a great investigator. She tracked me down and knew most of my story already. She told me what David's been doing to Cynthia Webber and her family. We need to arrest this asshole."

"We?" Detective Bain raised his eyebrows again.

"Well, I may not be on the force anymore, but I've got a booming PI business down in Denver. Any information I have on Jerew is yours if it will help get him arrested."

"Detective Bain?" a voice came from the office intercom. "I'm sorry to interrupt, but there's a gentleman here who says he needs to see you. He said he'll wait all night if he has to."

"Any idea what it's about?" Detective Bain eyed Kat as he waited for a reply.

"He says he wants to turn himself in. Apparently, he's been stealing from his employer."

"Okay. Not exactly high priority but I'll see if I can fit him in. We're just about done here."

"You should know that he seems somewhat intoxicated and claims the information he has to share with you relates to the David Jerew case."

"You know what? Why don't you send him on back?"

"Yes, sir."

"This ought to be interesting." Detective Bain looked at Kat as she moved her chair to make room for their guest.

"Did you want me to leave?" Kat asked Detective Bain.

"Not a chance. If this is about David Jerew, then I could use your insights."

59

Goddammit, this better work! Cynthia thought to herself on her way to pick up Linda. She had contacted April who was willing to lend Cynthia her car as a way to lure David into their meeting. April wanted to help more, but given she was out on bail, she was nervous about getting herself into more trouble and Cynthia understood. Together, Cynthia and Linda had hatched a cunning plan. They would use April's car with Linda in the driver's seat. Linda was about the same size as April, and they both had long hair. It was dark, and as long as they didn't park under a street light, nobody would be the wiser that it wasn't April sitting in the car.

Cynthia was going to get out of the car and try and get David talking—to admit that he'd forced Gord to steal from PPC and that he'd falsified the ethics complaint against her to CPA. Linda was going to outfit Cynthia with a mini-mic, and she would record David and Cynthia's conversation from inside April's Hyundai. Cynthia arrived at the news station in record time, and Linda was ready to go.

"Did you remember the mic?" Cynthia asked as soon as Linda jumped in the car.

"Of course. Right here," Linda said, holding up her bag.

"And you've got all the recording equipment you need?"

"All I need is my phone. They're amazing little tools, you know. The mic is wireless and sends the recording signal directly to the app on my phone. Piece of cake."

"Nice. Is there anything else we need?"

"I sure hope not. How much time do we have?"

"I told him one hour, and that was about thirty minutes ago. By the time we get to the university, we should still have fifteen minutes to get ready before he shows up." Cynthia glanced at the clock on the dash of April's Hyundai. "Shit. You know what. This guy is really obsessed with his daughter. Maybe we should set up now before we drive to the school. It would be just our luck that he'd be there waiting for us when we got there."

"Good idea," Linda said, digging in her bag and pulling out the microphone. "If we clip the mic here, on your collar, your hair will keep it hidden, and it won't affect the sound."

"What if a wind comes up? Won't you be able to see the mic then?"

"Maybe. Okay, let's put it on the inside collar of your coat but down far enough you won't see it if the collar flaps open." Linda pulled out her phone and selected the recording app. "Say something. I want to make sure the mic will pick up your voice."

"Hellooo-oooo. I feel weird."

"It's okay. That did the trick. Are you ready to get this dick to spill?"

"So ready. We need to switch places. Remember, you're April, not Linda."

"Right. Let's do it." Linda and Cynthia jumped out of the Hyundai, ran around the front, hive-fiving as they passed each other and got back in the car. Linda put the car in gear and headed towards the university.

"Shit. Are you going to be able to call the cops and use your recording app at the same time?" Cynthia didn't want to miss their chance to get David behind bars.

"I'm not sure. I've never tried that before. Leave your phone, and I'll call the detective with your phone and then we know for sure the recording is still good."

"Good idea." Cynthia took a deep breath and let it out slowly, trying to calm her nerves as they got closer to the university.

She had to believe David wanted to meet with his daughter more than he valued his freedom.

* * *

"Detective Bain, this is Gordon James, CFO of Prairie Pipeline Company." The station receptionist introduced Gord from the doorway. From the looks of Gord, "somewhat intoxicated" was putting it mildly. He looked like he was about to fall over if he didn't get a seat quickly and he reeked of scotch.

"Hello, Mr. James. Please have a seat." Detective Bain motioned towards the empty chair in front of his desk. "This is my associate, Kat Wilde. Anything you have to say you can say in front of her."

Gord leaned over and stretched his hand out to Kat. "Nice to meet you," he said slurring his words. Kat shook Gord's hand.

"What brings you in tonight, Mr. James?" Detective Bain got right to the point.

"Well, I apologize, sir, I made an appointment to see you tomorrow, but I just can't wait that long. I've done a terrible thing."

"Do you mind if I record this conversation?" Detective Bain was confused. He thought Gord was here to share information about David. Gord nodded in approval, and Detective Bain pressed record.

"Interview with Gordon James. Saturday, January 6, 2018, 8:10 p.m. Katrina Wilde and Detective Randy Bain present. Please continue, Mr. James."

"I stole from my employer," Gord broke down in drunken tears as he described how he'd been stealing from PPC for years. "I was scared. I wanted a clean audit report, so I did what he said."

"Who are you referring to, Mr. James?"

"David Jerew, partner at Darlington & Associates. He's our auditor. Prairie Pipeline Company's auditor."

"What exactly did Mr. Jerew say to you?"

"He told me that PPC was a company that attracted a lot of controversy, given what we do. He told me it was risky for him to take on such a client and if I wanted to come out clean as a whistle, he was going to need something from me." Gord took a minute and put his elbow on Detective Bain's desk, resting his head against his hand. He closed his eyes. "Is the room spinning?"

"No, Mr. James. Are you okay to continue?"

"Ah . . . yeah. Uh, what was I saying?" Kat noticed Gord was now sweating profusely and his skin looked clammy.

"Maybe we should continue this when you feel better?" Kat suggested. "I'm sure Detective Bain has a place you can lay down for a while." She glanced at the detective, and he nodded in agreement.

"We have an empty cell. We can get you a warm blanket and some water. When you feel better, we can continue this conversation."

"David Jerew threatened my career if I didn't pay him. He insisted on cash. He told me nobody would ever notice." Gord sobbed, his head in his hands. Kat and Randy looked at each other.

"Help me get him into the drunk tank." Randy moved around to the front of his desk and grabbed Gord under his right armpit while Kat flung Gord's left arm over her neck, grabbed his left wrist and put her right arm around his waist. The two of them simultaneously pulled Gord to his feet and walked him a short distance down the hall to the cell reserved for the drunks. They searched Gord for anything he might be able to use to harm himself and took his belt and wallet to be held as personal effects at reception.

Randy heard his name down the hall.

"Detective Bain . . . Detective Bain, you have an urgent phone call from Linda Reeves, the reporter."

"Thanks, Wanda. I'll take it in my office."

60

As Linda and Cynthia pulled into the university parking lot closest to the environmental sciences building, there was no trace of David anywhere. There were no other vehicles in the parking lot. Linda scanned the parking lot for a darker area that still had an easy escape route.

"There he is," Linda said nodding her head in the direction of a street lamp halfway across the parking lot.

"I wonder what he did with his vehicle?" Cynthia mused out loud. "Don't get too close. Remember, we want him to think you're April, so it's best if he can't see you very well. What about over there?"

"I think that looks perfect. You ready for this? I'll call Detective Bain as soon as you're out of the car. I'm going to leave it running just in case we need to get out of here fast, or I need to run his ass over." Cynthia chuckled at the protectiveness of her friend.

"Hopefully that won't be necessary. Alright, David, time to admit what you've done." Cynthia took a deep breath. "Here we go." She got out of the car and started walking towards David. She started out slowly at first to give Linda time to call Detective Bain but then David started walking towards her and she decided should she walk a little faster, so they would meet farther away from the vehicle.

It had been snowing gently for the last hour or so, and the parking lot was a little slippery. The snowflakes seemed to get bigger as Cynthia got closer to David.

"Where's April?" David said once Cynthia was in earshot.

"In the car."

"That wasn't part of the plan. I want to talk to my daughter."

"You'll get your chance." Cynthia was trying to act naturally and not talk directly into the microphone that was hidden just inside her coat. "She wanted to make sure you weren't going to try anything funny. Can you blame her? After everything that's happened in the last couple of days? I'm questioning my own sanity at this point. You're a dangerous man."

"I told you, once my story comes out, you're going to be the one who is wanted. Maybe not by the police, but you'll never work as a CPA."

"And that's because I stole from your client?"

"I'm glad you're finally coming around, Ms. Webber. Now, let me see my daughter." David started walking towards the Hyundai, but Cynthia stood her ground.

"And how exactly did I steal from PPC? I'm curious how you see this going down."

"You threatened Gord James and his career until he broke down and found a way to hide the stolen money in the bookkeeping."

"I'm flattered you think I have the power to threaten Gord James. Nobody's going to believe I could do anything to hurt his career. I'm an accounting student for crying out loud."

"True, but *I'm* a pretty powerful man in this town."

"So, now you admit that *you're* the one who coerced Gord into stealing from PPC?"

"Gord and I had a good thing going until you and your boyfriend had to interfere." Cynthia tried to remain expressionless. She didn't want David to know Ben had helped her uncover the missing money.

"What are you talking about? I don't have a boyfriend."

"My mistake," David said coolly. "Enough chit-chat, Ms. Webber. I'm ready to see my daughter now." David started walking towards the Hyundai. Cynthia walked after him, trying to think of something to prevent him from getting to the car.

Linda had been watching the exchange between David and Cynthia very closely. Why isn't Detective Bain here yet? She could see David was headed her way, and her heart rate increased as she realized David was about to uncover the truth—April wasn't in the car. Linda locked the doors and looked around the vehicle for anything she could use to help. She found a toque, put it on, and pulled it down over eyes. She turned her body, so she was facing away from the window just as David arrived at the car. David tried the handle. No luck.

"Come on, April. I just want to talk to you. Open the door." Linda shook her head from inside the vehicle which, to her benefit, had fogged up a little. David kicked the tire and pounded the window with his fist. Cynthia arrived at the car, and she was about to say something to David when he started yelling at the woman he thought was April.

"Do you have any idea how much I've done for you?" Linda tried hard not to blow her cover which was apparently working pretty well. She was sure the kinds of things David had done for April weren't what normal fathers did, considering the restraining order April had against David. "You always were a spoiled little shit. I heard you and your boyfriend talking about how you accidentally killed Jim Dunn. I thought he was going to get you put in jail, so I got rid of him for you. Turns out you wanted to go to jail. My daughter, the do-gooder. Aren't you going to say anything? I had a man killed for you."

"Noooo!" A gut-wrenching scream came from behind Cynthia. It was April, and she was charging towards them with Eve following close behind her.

"April, stop! You're out on bail. Don't do anything you'll regret," Eve warned.

"What the fuck?! If you're here, then who's in your car? Don't tell me it's that bitch reporter?" David was clearly beyond agitated at this point, and a little light bulb seemed to flash behind his eyes. He pulled out his gun and pointed it at Cynthia.

"What are you up to, Ms. Webber? Whatever it is, you won't get away with it." The police were close enough that everyone in the parking lot could hear them now. Finally, Cynthia thought.

Just as David was distracted by the sirens, Linda opened the driver's side door of the Hyundai with enough force to knock David down and cause his gun to go flying. She pulled the car forward, rolled down the window and motioned for Cynthia, April, and Eve to get in. Cynthia and Eve had to drag April into the car. She was so overcome with rage and disbelief over what her father had done that she was catatonic.

Linda pulled the car up to where David was and tried to cut him off. A police car entered the parking lot from the opposite side. It was Detective Bain and Kat.

"There he is," Kat said, pointing across the parking lot. With sirens blazing, Detective Bain pulled up to where Linda had cornered David with April's Hyundai. David found a way between the vehicles and was starting to make a run for it when Detective Bain hopped out of the cruiser and ran after David. As luck would have it, the snow was really coming down, hiding any icy patches underfoot. David tried to turn the corner onto a pathway leading across campus when his foot gave out underneath him. Detective Bain was on him like a dog on his bone. Cynthia and Linda were standing outside the Hyundai, Linda still recording everything through the mic on Cynthia's jacket.

In less than three minutes, Detective Bain had arrested David and read him his rights. He put him in the back of the cruiser and turned to Cynthia and Linda.

"I'll need all of you down at the station to give statements," he said authoritatively. "I hope you realize how much danger you put yourselves in tonight. Is everyone alright in there?"

"We're all fine. At least we're physically fine," Linda added. "I'm sure the psychological damage will last longer than any of us would like. We'll see you at the station." Inside the cruiser, Kat couldn't resist baiting David. She turned around to face him.

"Do I look familiar to you?" she asked.

"Well, I never forget a pretty face." David was as cocky as ever even though he was in the back of a police cruiser with his hands in cuffs. "I don't think we've met before."

"Are you sure? Think back to a lonely night about seven years ago when you tried to hire a prostitute. My hair was blonde then. Things didn't go your way, so you ended up beating and raping me instead. I always knew you'd get what was coming to you. I never thought it would take this long though." Kat turned around, satisfied by the look of recognition and shock on David's face.

61

Down at the station, Gord was passed out in his cell. Randy and Kat decided it would be better to put David in his own cell, at least until they were able to hear Gord's allegations against him. Of course, David protested the entire time about how he'd done nothing wrong. April, Eve, Cynthia, and Linda waited out front until the detective was ready to hear their statements. April hadn't said a word since her outburst at the university. Eve was worried about her.

"April, are you alright?" April looked up at Eve with a hollow look in her eyes.

"My father hired a hitman to kill my boyfriend. And he thought he was protecting me. I don't think I'll ever be alright again." April laid her head on Eve's shoulder. Eve put her arm around her.

"What were you guys doing at the university?" Linda couldn't turn off her investigative instincts.

"April wanted to make sure David was arrested. There was no way I was letting her go there alone. We were watching from inside the building, but as soon as April saw David, she wanted to be able to hear what was going on, so we snuck down to the entryway. We could hear most of David and Cynthia's conversation, so we'll be able to corroborate your story."

"I think we recorded it all."

"What?! That's a little risky isn't it?" Eve was surprised Cynthia and Linda would take a chance like that.

"I'm a reporter. It's what I do."

"Right." Their conversation was interrupted when Cynthia got called to Detective Bain's office. Cynthia followed the receptionist down the hall to the detective's office. Cynthia took a seat in front of Randy's desk.

"You've been through a lot this last week, Ms. Webber. I won't keep you long. I'm sure you want to get back to your family. If you could tell me what happened tonight, I'm happy to let you go on your way." Detective Bain took a sip of the coffee Wanda had delivered when she brought Cynthia in. Cynthia proceeded to recount her version of the night's events for Detective Bain.

"Thank you, Ms. Webber; you can send Dr. Greenwich in." Randy was eager to get home himself, but he knew the paperwork would have him at the station until well into the night.

"Actually, Detective, there's something else. Along with two of my colleagues, I discovered Mr. Jerew has been bribing a client of his for the last several years."

"Can you tell me who the client is?"

"Gord James, CFO of Prairie Pipeline Company. Mr. Jerew threatened the only way PPC would receive a clean audit report was if he was paid, off-the-record, in cash. My colleagues and I found proof in PPC's bookkeeping. Mr. James was stealing money from the shareholders, and Mr. Jerew admitted it tonight. There's a recording of our conversation. I believe Mr. James paid him cash and possibly used it to hire someone to kill Kurt Ripple. My friend Linda, I mean, Miss Reeves, has a photograph of Mr. Jerew and Mr. James exchanging an envelope. I would imagine it contained a whole lot of cash. This year's bribe payment."

"Well, Mr. James is currently in our custody, and as soon as he sobers up, I will be talking with him. He did mention he'd been stealing from PPC and couldn't live with the guilt anymore. Do you remember how this works from when you gave your statement when you found Jim Dunn's body? I'm sure you do. It was only a few days ago. We'll get this typed up and have you sign it when it's ready. It will likely be sometime in the morning."

"Thank you, Detective. I'll send Dr. Greenwich in."

"Thank you, Ms. Webber. Oh, I'll need that recording."

"I'll make sure Linda gets it to you as soon as possible." Cynthia headed down the hall to the reception area where the other ladies were waiting.

"Dr. Greenwich, Detective Bain would like to see you. His office is at the end of the hall and to the right." Eve stood up and looked at April.

"Do you want to come with me? I don't want to leave you here."

"We'll take care of her while you're gone," Cynthia volunteered. "It's funny. This is where I met the two of you, and here we are again." Cynthia sat down next to April just as her cell phone went off. Not wanting to be rude and talk in front of everyone, Cynthia decided to step outside to answer.

"Keep an eye on her. I'll be right back," Cynthia said to Linda as she left. "Hello?"

"Cynthia, it's Ben."

"Hi, Ben."

"I wanted to let you know that Sam and I filed the ethics complaint against David, and Sam wants me to go with him to HR on Monday. He feels like he should resign his position at D&A because he didn't push David enough for an explanation when it came to the shareholder loans each year. Not having the shareholders sign off certainly would lead someone to question whether the information contained in the files could be false and misleading."

"Thanks for filing the ethics complaint. Apparently, David filed one against me, so I'm glad the one against him is on record now."

"What?! That's ridiculous."

"Yeah, well, he's been arrested now, so hopefully we won't have to worry about him for a long time. Good luck with HR. I hope Sam doesn't resign."

"Me too. He's pretty upset about the whole thing. Feels like he wasn't doing his job as manager to the best of his abilities. What happened with David?"

"It's a bit of a long story, and I'm still at the station. Could I tell you about it tomorrow?"

"Of course. Why don't we get some dinner on Monday and I can tell you how it went with HR too?"

"Sure. Call me when you're done work."

"You got it."

"Thanks, Ben. I appreciate all your help with this. I know I still owe you a study session."

"All in good time. I'm not going anywhere."

"Alright, I'll talk to you tomorrow." Cynthia clicked off her phone and set it to vibrate. She walked back into the police station as Eve was coming down the hall from Detective Bain's office.

"I swear I just saw Gord James in the holding cell next to Jerew. Busy place tonight."

"You did." Cynthia paused, not sure if she was supposed to repeat what Detective Bain had told her, but she thought he probably wouldn't have mentioned anything if she wasn't supposed to know. "Apparently he came to turn himself in for something." Cynthia decided not to give up everything she knew, just in case. Eve didn't want to admit she had tried to wake Gord up when she walked by his cell.

Linda was next up to be questioned. Eve suggested to Detective Bain that he wouldn't get many details out of April as she seemed to be processing everything. The most horrific being that her father is a murderer. He had always been a terrible dad, and she knew he'd been stalking her for weeks, but she never thought he'd go this far. April felt like she could have stopped Kurt's murder had she reported David's restraining order violation weeks ago. Then David never would have been around to hear her and Kurt talking about Jim's death.

Once Linda was finished talking with the detective, and on her way back to the reception area, April stood up.

"I'll be right back she said," heading down the hall. Instead of turning towards Detective Bain's office, she turned the opposite way towards the holding cells. She found her father in his cell.

April whispered through the bars at her estranged father. "I will never understand why you did what you did. In a way, Kurt was a lot like you. As much as it pains me to say it. He didn't want me to go to the police either. It's a good thing my mother knew right from wrong and was there to teach me which was which. I could almost understand you following me around, but this . . ." April started to cry as she remembered Kurt and Jim, and all the emotions she felt when she found out the man she had accidentally hit with her shoe was dead. "This time you've crossed a line you can never come back over. I will make sure nobody knows we are related. Ever! You are dead to me." David started to speak in response, but April was gone as quickly as she had arrived.

When she got back to the reception area, Eve asked April if she was alright.

"I will be," April whispered. "I just had to get something off my chest." The women left the police station together. Eve offered to drive April's car since she was still concerned about her. She planned to take April to the hospital just to be safe. Cynthia and Linda offered to go with them, but Eve told them it wasn't necessary. She drove Linda and Cynthia to S-CAL where both their vehicles were. Linda was feeling guilty for being so hard on Eve during her past interviews. Eve had certainly shown she had a soft, caring side tonight.

"Thanks for your help, Dr. Greenwich. And thanks for the ride. I'm sorry I'm so hard on you sometimes. In my job, I have to stay objective no matter how many sides of the story there are. I'm just as hard on the big oil giants too."

"I understand, Ms. Reeves. You have a job to do. And you're very good at it, but I also have a job to do. One that could improve this city, in my opinion."

"Of course. If I can ever help with that, please let me know." Linda extended a hand to Eve which she accepted and shook.

"You'll be hearing from me."

"I look forward to it." Cynthia and Linda got out of the car. Both women were happy yet drained. Cynthia looked at her best friend, a smirk appearing on her face.

"You're going in there to write this story, aren't you?"

"Can you blame me? It's quite the story. The life of a reporter means you don't get to sleep when you're tired. Especially when there's news to report."

"Haha, I knew it! Be careful."

"Don't worry. Security is still here, and Kat is coming out to go over her story with me. She's ready to go public. She feels like her part of David's story will add fuel to the fire and make sure he stays locked up for a long time."

"Wow. Well, I guess I'll see you on the news then. If I hurry home, I might get to see Luke before he goes to bed."

"Give him a hug from Auntie Linda. Your mom too."

"You got it. Thanks for your help tonight. I wouldn't have had that recording without you. It's evidence now."

"Anytime, my friend." Linda and Cynthia hugged, and Cynthia got in her car and watched while Linda entered the news station. Cynthia was happy to head home and put this crazy week behind her.

62

"Mom!" Cynthia barged into her parents' house excited to tell Gayle that David was behind bars. "We got him!"

"Cynthia? What's going on?" Gayle came out from down the hall.

"David's in jail. He won't be bothering us anymore. Luke and I can go back home."

"Well, you know you are welcome here as long as you like, but that is great news. I have some more great news. The hospital called while you were out, and your dad can come home in the morning."

"Mama!" Luke came running from the bathroom where he'd been getting ready for bed and jumped into Cynthia's arms.

"Hey, buddy! Mom, that *is* great news. Did I miss story time?"

"No. Grandma and I were just about to read *Guess How Much I Love You.*" As Luke said the name of the book, he couldn't help but stretch his arms out wide as if to say, "This much." Gayle gave Cynthia a sheepish grin as she knew Luke should be in bed by now.

"My favourite," Cynthia said, stretching her arms out like her son. Cynthia, Gayle, and Luke all sat down on the couch, and Cynthia read the book. She tucked Luke into bed then went to the kitchen to make some tea.

"So, what's the plan now?" asked Gayle.

"I really should get back to studying for that final exam. It's a few months away, but I know it will be here before I know it. I should probably start looking for a job too. I think it's time to start fresh. Maybe D&A's not the best place for me even with David out of the picture."

"You'll do fine on your exam, dear. And you've never had a problem finding work. I meant what's the plan tonight? You must be exhausted."

"Oh," Cynthia laughed and hugged Gayle. "I *am* exhausted. I think I'll drink my tea in the bath and go to bed. How early can we get Dad tomorrow?"

"They want the doctor to check him one last time during rounds in the morning, but I think it's safe to say we could get him before breakfast."

"Good, let's do that. I think a celebratory breakfast is in order. Love you, Mom."

"Love you too, Cyn."

* * *

"I really appreciate you doing this." Linda walked Kat out to her car after interviewing her and chatting about her life in Denver.

"No problem. It's important that people know David didn't just snap, and that he's had a history of bribery and much, much worse crimes."

"It's shocking, really, the secrets people keep. The piece should be live first thing in the morning if you want to watch it."

"I think I've re-lived this nightmare enough." Kat glanced down at the ground and back up at Linda. "Thank you, Miss Reeves."

"So, what's next? Are you headed back to Denver tomorrow?"

"I am. Randy wanted me to stay. He even offered me a detective position with the force."

"Wow," Linda arched her eyebrows in surprise.

"I belong in Denver. I love my PI business. It's a different way I can help bring down the bad guys."

"Thank you again for helping Cynthia and me. This really shows David's true nature and establish his pattern of corrupt behaviour. Take care."

"Take care." Kat raised her hand in a quick goodbye, gave a little smile, and turned towards her rental car.

* * *

April and Eve sat together in the hospital waiting room. April had her elbows on her knees and her head between her hands. She looked up at Eve, unsure if she should say anything.

"Did you know that guy?" April asked Eve.

"Which guy?"

"The drunk at the police station. That CFO."

"I know him very well, actually. We've been having an affair for the last six months." Eve looked down at the ground. It felt strange to say it out loud.

"Does your husband know?"

"No, he never suspected an affair. It doesn't matter though. Our marriage was in trouble long ago. He actually believed I killed that controller. He believed the news reports without even listening to my side of the story. What kind of husband does that?"

"Will you tell him about the affair?"

"I don't really see the point. It feels like things are over between us anyway. He told me not to come home after I was released from jail."

"Will you move in with your boyfriend? I'm sorry. I shouldn't be asking you so many personal questions."

"It's okay. No, Gord isn't the one for me. We had a lot of fun, but it's time for me to take a break from men for a while. Plus, I'm going to have to figure out what it means to be separated, I guess. The kids will need me. I'll need them."

"If there's anything I can do at work to help you out, just say the word. You've done so much for me and my career." April seemed to be returning to her old self.

"Thanks, April."

63

Cynthia woke up earlier than she had all week. It would be at least another hour before the sun was up. She was excited to see her dad come home from the hospital. She tiptoed out of the guest room where Luke was still sleeping. Her textbooks were still in the bag she'd packed when they left her place seeking safety from David. Now was as good a time as any to get back to studying for her final CPA exam.

She sat down on the living room floor, using the coffee table as a desk and opened her book. It was so quiet Cynthia could hear the kitchen clock ticking. She picked up the TV remote and pressed the red button. She saw Linda standing in front of the police station.

"City police prison guard, Mark Morgan, was doing morning rounds when he discovered the body." What now, Cynthia wondered, her eyes glued to the TV. "David Jerew was found dead, hanging in his cell at approximately 3 a.m. this morning. It appears he fashioned a noose from a blanket then hung himself from the pipes that feed the sprinkler system. What's unclear at this point is how Jerew managed to pull this off without the guard hearing or seeing him."

"Cynthia?" Cynthia jumped at the sound of her name. She turned around and saw Gayle standing behind her.

"Hi, Mom," Cynthia whispered. "David hung himself."

"I'm not surprised. That man was deeply disturbed."

"True. I guess I didn't think he would do something as

drastic as ending his own life."

"The actions he's taken up to this point have been pretty drastic, Cyn." Cynthia let out an ironic grunt.

"I guess you just never know. Anyway, you must be even more excited to see Dad than I am. I know we're going to get breakfast after we get Dad but how about some tea?"

"I am, and that sounds wonderful."

* * *

Cynthia and her family headed to her dad's favourite diner to celebrate his release from the hospital. He ordered his favourite breakfast—blueberry pancakes with bacon and eggs.

"I sure did miss all of you while I was in the hospital." Bob held his coffee up as a nod to his family then took a big sip.

"We missed you too, Dad." Cynthia's phone went off as she was about to "cheers" his coffee cup. She looked at the call display. "It's Detective Bain. I better answer. Excuse me," she said, getting up from the table and heading outside.

"Hello, this is Cynthia."

"Hi, Cynthia. It's Randy Bain. I wanted to make sure you saw the news about David Jerew."

"Yes, I saw that he hung himself. I guess that means he won't be able to hurt anyone ever again." Cynthia wasn't sure what to think. This past week had been unbelievable.

"I know this is out of the blue but, I wanted to ask you if you'd be interested in working for us?"

"At the police station? You need an accountant?"

"Our financial crimes department is swamped. I think you'd be a natural there."

"Oh, wow! You know I'm not a CPA yet, right?" Cynthia felt her heart pump with the excitement of a job prospect.

"That's fine. We have a forensic accountant on staff. I've already talked to her, and she's more than happy to show you the ropes especially since she'll be getting the extra help she needs. She'd love it if you could start as soon as possible."

"Really? Um . . ." Cynthia was overwhelmed at the thought of the opportunity. She didn't know the first thing about forensic accounting, but she was excited to learn.

"Why don't I give you until Wednesday to give me a decision?" Randy sensed Cynthia's hesitation and didn't want to scare her off. "You've been through a lot this last week. Take some time and think it over."

"I will. Thank you, Detective." Cynthia put her phone in her purse and hurried inside to be with her family. She sat down at the table, her face white as a ghost.

"What's wrong, dear," Gayle asked nervously.

"I think I just got a job. Detective Bain needs someone in the financial crimes department."

"That's great news! I told you you wouldn't have any trouble finding a job. You didn't even have to look." Gayle and Bob raised their coffee mugs at the same time.

"To Cyndi's new job," they said in unison.

"Yay, Mommy," Luke added.

"Thanks, guys. What a week." Cynthia took a sip of her tea and thought about Ben and how she couldn't wait to tell him the news as soon as she got home.

64

It was Monday evening, and Cynthia and Ben had agreed to meet at Ben's apartment after work and walk to the pub down the street for dinner. Ben was still getting ready when Cynthia arrived. This time he was the one that was nervous. He had just changed his shirt for the second time when Cynthia knocked on his door. He rushed to open it.

"Hi. Come in," he said. Good one Ben, real original. "How was your day?"

"It was a lot of fun. I'm going to miss spending so much time with Luke when I start working again."

"So, you decided to take Detective Bain up on his offer?" Ben asked, remembering their conversation yesterday.

"Yeah. I did a bit of research into what a forensic accountant does, and I think with my background in auditing, it will make a great next step. Could be pretty interesting too. Maybe Linda can show me how she honed her amazing investigative skills." Ben chuckled while he grabbed his coat from the back of the door.

"Shall we?" Ben held the door open for Cynthia then closed the door behind them. Ben locked the door, and Cynthia started to walk down the hall. Ben grabbed her arm and turned her towards him. "There's something I've been meaning to do for a while now," he said as he brushed Cynthia's hair away from her face. Cynthia wanted to ask what, but it was clear what the answer was. Ben softly planted his lips on Cynthia's and kissed her slowly while running his fingers through her hair. Cynthia melted into Ben, enjoying every second. Ben looked into Cynthia's eyes and said, "Now that we got that out of the way, we can enjoy our evening," and gave her his classic wink. Cynthia couldn't help but giggle.

It was a clear and surprisingly mild night for January, so the pair enjoyed their short walk to the pub. They chose a corner table and ordered a couple of drinks.

"I'm dying to know how the meeting went with HR today? Is Sam still a D&A employee?"

"Yes! And it went really well. HR was impressed with Sam coming forward and sharing what he'd suspected the last few years. They actually took some responsibility as well."

"Really? I'm not sure I understand," Cynthia squinted a puzzled look at Ben.

"They felt like they haven't had proper procedures in place to help employees feel comfortable coming forward with information that could be detrimental to another employee's career. Staffing has exploded so much in the last few years they haven't had time to focus on informing employees about what to do in these situations." Ben took a sip of his beer. "So, Sam will be working in close partnership with HR to design a program to educate employees about how to come forward when they're unsure if any ethical principles have been ignored."

"Like a whistleblower program?" Cynthia asked.

"Sort of. Part of it will include educating employees more about the CPA code of ethical principles and the other major part will be the steps to take in the case of a violation by themselves or another employee." Ben saw Cynthia had her hand on the table and reached across the table to hold it. "I think Sam was pretty relieved."

"I bet. I'm glad he didn't get fired, and this program sounds like a good thing for D&A. So, what are you going to order?" Cynthia flashed a smile at Ben who blushed and smiled back.

65

Three Months Later . . .

"I'm so glad you suggested this, it's the perfect way to celebrate," Cynthia smiled at Ben as she sat down on the couch, a cool glass of white wine in her hand. Chinese takeout sat neatly on the coffee table in front of her, waiting to be unwrapped. Two plates in hand, Ben entered the living room via the dining area from his tiny apartment-sized kitchen. Living on the seventh floor of a 42-floor building had its perks, but a massive kitchen wasn't one of them. Still, it suited Ben just fine; he ate out or at the office most of the time anyway.

"Did you see the *Focus* magazine?" Ben asked Cynthia as he sat down next to her, put the two plates on the coffee table, and grabbed the magazine from the end table. The magazine was folded open to the gold medal winners of the Comprehensive Final Examination. The award was given to the top three marks earned each time the exam was written. There was Cynthia, featured along with two men from Deloitte.

"I still don't believe it," she said. "There must have been a miscount."

"You deserve it. You worked so hard for it. Cynthia Webber, CPA."

"With everything that's happened in the last few weeks, I thought for sure I was going to forget everything I learned. It's ironic, since David threatened I'd never work as an accountant, and he was the one who would have ended up losing his license had he not killed himself."

"Let's not talk about him right now. The damage is done, and he won't be hurting anyone ever again."

"You're right, let's not talk about him. I'm so thankful for your help, though."

Booonnggggg-ooonnggggg! A loud gonging sound vibrated the railing of the balcony outside. Cynthia and Ben could hear the vibrations as they bewilderedly looked at each other and towards the balcony.

"Did you hear that?" Cynthia asked puzzled. She couldn't help feeling on edge considering the events of the past few months.

"Yeah, but what was it? I've never heard anything like that. Like someone took a large sledgehammer and smacked it against the balcony railing. My ears are still ringing." Ben got up and hurried towards the balcony doors as Cynthia braced herself on the couch, fearful that someone was outside. She knew this was impossible. How on earth would they get up here? Ben slid the glass door open as the full-length curtains followed him out onto the balcony. Obviously seeing nothing, he leaned over to have a look below.

All Cynthia could hear from inside Ben's apartment was, "What the fff . . .?" Cynthia jumped off the couch and started to call out to Ben, but he was already on his way back inside.

"Don't go out there."

"Why not? What's going on? Did something hit the balcony?" All the colour had drained out of Ben's face, and Cynthia could tell he was processing what he had seen below. Slowly Ben started to speak.

"I think . . . it's . . . a body."

ABOUT THE AUTHOR

Michelle Cornish self-published *Keep More Money: Find an Accountant You Trust to Help You Grow Your Small Business, Increase Profit, and Save Tax* in February 2017 to help entrepreneurs find a trustworthy accountant. *Keep More Money* is all about asking the right questions to find the right professional for the job.

After publishing *Keep More Money*, Michelle realized what she really wanted to do was write stories. Feeling like there just aren't enough books with accountants as protagonists, Michelle's idea for *Murder Audit* was born! Why should lawyers get to have all the fun?!!

Learn more about Michelle at www.michellecornish.com.

CPSIA information can be obtained
at www.ICGtesting.com
Printed in the USA
LVHW032032021118
595813LV00001B/32